Cupcakes And Corpses

A Terrified Detective Mystery

Cover Design: Kathleen Baldwin
Formatting by Ink Lion Books

Chapter One

"Claire, could you get that?" Gino, my father's second cousin and my employer, was holding a chocolate covered doughnut in one hand and a Styrofoam cup of coffee in the other.

I sighed to myself and picked up the phone. "Francini Private Investigation Agency. You think you've got a problem? Talk to us." I swear my brain shrunk every time I had to make that announcement. Needless to say, the greeting was Gino's idea and nothing I could say would persuade him to change it.

He wanted things the way they had been when he left Cleveland to soak up the Miami sun and turned the agency over to me. Despite what he wanted, things weren't the same. I now had three murder investigations under my belt and didn't want to return to sorting mail, answering calls, and occasionally taking pictures of spouses who were where they shouldn't have been with people they shouldn't have been with. I wanted to be a private investigator. Sure, I'm terrified, but I'm good at it. And I helped people.

Instead, after swearing I wouldn't fall back into this career dead-end, here I was at 31, almost 32, eking out a living. The caller yelled for Gino so, figuring he was a bill collector or irate customer, I handed the phone over.

My boss' mouth was still half-full and chocolate frosting hung from his bushy gray-black mustache. "Timothy. Calm down. I'll bet your sister is fine. Maybe she don't want to talk to you." Gino took a swallow of his coffee as he listened. He bounced his hand up and down as if he was playing with a basketball. "Okay, okay. I'll send my assistant to her house. See what's up. We'll call you when we know something."

I motioned to Gino to see if we'd get paid for this. He shook his head. "Don't worry, Timothy. It's on the house."

I blew out a deep breath. I had hoped, by working both here and part time at *Cannoli's*, my Aunt Lena's bakery, I could eventually earn enough to start my own PI agency. Gino had been back for three months and so far hadn't been able to give me the raise he promised when I agreed to stay on here. Whenever I brought up the subject of my pay increase, he would turn his pockets inside out and tell me how broke he was. If he continued to do favors for people like Timothy, I'd never be anything more than a paper-pusher.

I zoned back as Gino was returning the phone to me. "Here, Claire. Timothy is gonna give you his sister's address."

No surprise that I would be the one to check on the

woman. My resentment was flashing in my eyes, so I kept my head down, grabbed the phone, and took the information.

Timothy's sister, Eileen, lived in Cleveland's near West Side. It wouldn't take me long to get there and I thought about stopping for a chocolate cupcake and a cup of tea first.

Out of the side of his mouth, Gino muttered, "She's probably sleeping one off. I remember when we were kids. Me and Timothy would sneak a beer from her fridge. She never knew it. That woman could drink any man under the table."

"So you're saying it's okay for me to grab something to eat on my way to her house?"

"Yeah, sure." He pulled out a dollar. "It's on me."

In other circumstances I'd tell him to put his money away. A dollar wouldn't even cover the tea. My pride sulked but times were hard and I took what he offered.

Despite my stomach's growling, I drove straight to my assignment, freebie though it was. My conscientiousness often got me nothing but aggravation. If I was a betting woman this one would too. I couldn't help myself; the nuns at Holy Trinity elementary school taught me the sinfulness of procrastination.

I got to Eileen's 1930's bungalow-style home and rang the bell several times. No answer. I followed by rapping on the door until my fist turned red. Still no answer. I stepped back and was about to return to my car when a woman's voice stopped me.

"Excuse me, but are you looking for Eileen O'Donnell?" With a start, I found myself staring at a mail carrier. She was a bit on the plump side with tightly curled brown hair and her uniform stretched mercilessly across her hips and chest.

"Yes, I am. Have you seen her?"

"How do you know Eileen?"

"I don't. Her brother, Timothy, asked me to check on her."

"It's about time someone did." She frowned. "No, I haven't seen her and her mail is piling up. Eileen usually grabs her stuff before I even have a chance to close the mail slot. She hasn't been doing that for the past three days. Neighbors haven't seen her either." She waited, probably expecting me to say something. When I didn't, she continued. "I don't ordinarily do something like this, but I was thinking to call the cops. Let them snoop around. I just hope they find out she's okay."

While I didn't know US Postal Service policy, it sounded like a plan to me. A niggling voice in my brain stopped me from immediately saying so. Maybe I needed to get involved. Make the call myself. Yet I wasn't too excited about pursuing this. It wasn't my case. I wasn't getting paid as a PI anymore. Still, I felt like I had to say something. "If you're concerned, calling the police is probably the best thing you could do."

She glanced down the street. "Yeah, but I still have to deliver mail to the rest of the neighborhood. I could do it when I'm done. But you could call the cops now."

"Or I can wait until you get back." I didn't relish talking to the police about a woman who may just be away from home. All Gino told me to do was to see if Eileen was home. She apparently wasn't. End of my assignment. I refused to give a voice to my Catholic schoolgirl conscience to go above and beyond what Gino had asked.

The mail carrier's eyes narrowed. "I understand." The outrage in her voice indicated anything but understanding. "Don't get involved." She spun her two-wheeled bag of mail and stomped away.

Now I was ashamed, or embarrassed, or something and decided to take a look around. I began in the back of the house, opening the chain link gate. A doggy entrance had been cut out of the door. A dog the size of a Great Dane could probably fit through it.

The blood in my veins curdled. What if a big dog was inside? What if it was hungry? What if it mistook me for a rawhide chew? I was only 5'2" and 107 pounds. I couldn't fight it off.

I wanted to bolt. After all, that mail carrier would finish soon and she'd call the police. No involvement on my part necessary.

That's when I heard it. A soulful moan that played upon the fibers of my heart. Somebody was alive inside and probably hurt. I kicked the doggy door gently with the toe of my shoe. It gave way. Estimating the size, I determined that, while it'd be a tight squeeze, I could get through. Still I hesitated. Sure, the sound could be coming from Timothy's sister. It could also be coming from her famished and half-mad pit bull. *Weren't hungry dogs more vicious?*

Rather than being a complete coward, I stuck my head through the doggy door and looked around. I didn't see anything, but from the sound, whatever or whoever it turned out to be, was in the kitchen.

I clasped my arms to my body and tried to force my shoulders through the opening. Feeling as if I were a string of licorice, I twisted my upper body to the right and then the left. With one final effort, I pushed through the doggy entryway and managed to land on my forearms. My body was half in and half out. Upon taking a deep breath, the smell of something akin to rotted fruit assaulted me.

Then I saw the body. A woman, probably Eileen, lay sprawled out on the floor. Shards of broken glass were scattered around her. From the smell and the looks of her, she'd been dead at least a few days.

Her fuzzy, pink bathrobe was off her shoulders, exposing straps from her nightgown. The right one having slipped from her shoulder. Around her neck was a deep red velveteen ribbon tied into a big, droopy bow.

Lying with its head on its front paws was the producer of the sorrowful noise that drew me in. The puppy looked up at me as if to say, "Do something."

I backed my head out of the door with the speed of a lit firecracker, grabbed my phone and called 911. Sitting back on my heels, I described the state of Eileen's body.

And how she was gift-wrapped.

My nerves, already frayed a bit, almost unraveled with the 911 operator's response. In a voice that sounded like an adolescent, she said, "This is my first day on my own. Let me check and see what you're supposed to do now. Wait a minute. Are you sure she's dead?"

I huffed, "Yes! She's sprawled out on the linoleum, her head at an angle no live person could achieve. She's got a ribbon around her neck and her skin is pallid and bloated. She's dead all right."

"The police will be there shortly, so I want you to get inside the house and unlock the door for them."

"What?" I wanted to reach through the phone and throttle the woman. "What if the killer's still there?"

"I'll stay on the phone with you." Her voice sounding like she'd solved the problem.

Without my gun, which was back in my apartment, I was pretty defenseless. Except for my pepper spray. I pulled that out of my purse and held it tightly, just in case.

With the 911 operator's voice coming through my phone, I twisted and contorted until I'd squeezed all the way through the doggy door.

Although it was June, the weather didn't seem to know it and a cold front was keeping temperatures in the sixties. Even with a sweater on, I shivered. The temperature inside the house had to be in the forties.

The dog, with ears like a beagle but which looked part Boxer and who-knew-what else, turned its eyes to me again. I hoped it wasn't thinking my rear resembled a top sirloin.

Stepping around Eileen's body, I unlocked the front door and was set to wait. The dog's plight got to me and I wanted to at least give it some water, but I stopped myself. Doing something that simple could contaminate the crime scene.

Thank goodness it didn't take long for the police to arrive. I was less than surprised when I spotted Detective Brian Corrigan stepping through the door. Sometimes it seemed like he was the only detective in the Cleveland Police Department.

His blue eyes went from Eileen's body to me and back again. His voice was mock-serious. "Ms. DeNardo. Why is it, whenever there's any crime scene in the entire Cleveland Metropolitan area, there's a good chance you'll be involved? Do you use a Ouija board?"

We'd had similar conversations around corpses since I first got involved in murder cases. "That's not funny. This poor woman's brother is a friend of Gino's, and he was worried about her."

"Evidently not worried enough to visit her himself."

I wrapped my arms around myself. "You've got my statement. Can I go now?"

He closed his notebook. "Yeah. See you soon?"

My smile reached from ear to ear. Then quickly, I toned it down. After all, there was a dead body amongst us. "Before I go, can I give the dog some water?"

Corrigan glanced over at the mutt. "Animal Protective

League will be here soon. Go ahead, though. Poor guy's probably dehydrated." He called to one of the technicians for gloves and handed them to me.

The pup gave me a grateful look as he sopped up the liquid. I scratched him behind his floppy, brown ears and cooed to him, absent-mindedly hoping somebody would take him in.

My canine duty done, I left to go back to the office. As soon as I walked through the door, I filled Gino in. When I finished, he grabbed my hands and guided me to a chair. "Are you okay?"

Apparently Gino had forgotten this wasn't my first murder scene. Still I was touched that he was concerned about my well-being. "Did you already know about Eileen being dead? How did you find out?"

He waved his hand, as if my question had no bearing on the issue. "Police scanner. I got it just the other day. What's important is Timothy will be here in a minute. Have you thought of what you'll say to him?"

I had to close my gaping mouth. "Me? You're his friend. Or the police can tell him."

"Hello?" Timothy stumbled into the office as if he'd been suddenly awakened after an all-night bender. "I got here as soon as I got your message." His hair was sticking out everywhere. Gino flung one arm around Timothy and guy-hugged him. He bade him sit. Then in the wormy way I've seen him use during bad news times, Gino deferred to me. "This is Claire, my assistant. You've already talked on the phone. She's got news for you about your sister. Go ahead, Claire."

Timothy's expression reminded me of an animal with its foot caught in a trap. Already in pain and waiting only for the final assault. I glared at Gino before beginning.

I tried to keep my voice calm, gentle. "I regret to tell you your sister has passed away. The police will be contacting you soon with details." I didn't have the heart to say more. How do you tell someone their sister was murdered and tied up like a birthday present?

Timothy jumped from his chair. "How? When?"

To my relief, and, I'll admit, surprise, Gino took over. He placed his hand on his friend's shoulder and sympathy poured over his facial features. "Man, I'm so sorry. She was a good lady." He nodded toward the door and I understood he wanted me to leave. I was only too glad to give him and Timothy some privacy.

Thirty minutes later, Gino, his arm around Timothy's slumped shoulder joined me in the reception area. "Me and Timothy are going over to Players for a drink."

Timothy looked like he needed a friend even more than a drink. His eyes were red and his face, puffy.

Gino went on. "Lock up when you're done. See you tomorrow, Claire."

It was only three in the afternoon. Part of me thought of staying until five, just in case a new client came by. I almost chuckled at the absurdity of that happening. I decided to head home to get ready for my date with Corrigan. Surprisingly, Aunt Lena had given me the evening off. In the three months since her wedding, things between Corrigan and me had been heating up. My aunt wasn't above assisting in that push.

He and I'd come a long way from the first time we'd met over a dead body, one of my clients. One of the few benefits of no longer having my own PI business was, Corrigan and I no longer argued about my involvement in any murder case. A flash of melancholy for those former days shot through me.

Chapter Two

I had just put the finishing touches on my makeup when a knock at my door told me Corrigan had arrived. I took a deep breath and told him to come in.

Instead of it being the man I planned on swooping down on, it was Ed, or should I say, Uncle Ed. He'd been the lucky and brave man who married my feisty aunt. I'd known Ed before that, though. A part-time security guard, he had also worked on an as-needed basis for me. Smart, wiry, and savvy, he was invaluable. Since I'd lost the PI business, he spent more hours helping my aunt with *Cannoli's,* and from the appearance of the box he held, it looked as if he'd just come from there.

"Shouldn't leave your door open like that, Claire. Any crazy person could come inside."

"You sound like Aunt Lena." I smiled. "To what do I owe this visit?" I eyed the goodies he was holding.

"Brian is in the parking lot, so I'll keep it short. He's cooling his heels until I'm done telling you what I need to."

My heart revved up. “Is Aunt Lena okay?”

He gave me a crooked grin. “Better than okay. That is one fine woman. In fact, when she knew I was coming to see you, she asked me to bring you these.”

Inside the box was a luscious-looking cupcake with reddish frosting. I tilted my head in a question.

“Lena wants you to try it.”

“Now?”

“Yeah. She calls it a Strawberry dream. Tell me what you think so I can tell her. Then let’s talk about why I was coming here in the first place. It’s about that murder. The one where the sister of Gino’s pal bought it.”

I started to ask how he knew. Then I remembered. Ed was the original ‘I-know-a-guy-who-knows-a-guy.’

“Word travels. Anyway, I heard she worked at Smalley’s Chocolates for 20 years. The Smalley family is offering a reward to get the killer. Ten thousand dollars.”

My eyes opened so wide, my brows must have disappeared into my hairline. “That’s a down-payment on a PI business.” I put a lid on my excitement, waiting to hear more.

“Of course, you’ll want to hire me as your assistant when you start this new business.” He patted his slightly rounded belly. “I love Lena, but much more time at *Cannoli’s* and tasting her latest concoctions and I’ll lose my boyish figure for good.”

I chortled. That was one of the reasons I didn’t want to work full-time at *Cannoli’s.* I couldn’t afford to indulge all day long in my aunt’s heavenly éclairs, cakes, and assorted other goodies. I swear my body's fat cells swell just being in the vicinity of her pastry case.

But, for the sake of experimentation, I took a bite of the cupcake, closed my eyes, and let it melt in my mouth. It was life-changing. Strawberry frosting that gave way to a chocolate chip cupcake with a strawberry filling.

"What do you think, Claire?"

"It's delicious." My voice sounded dreamy even to me. "Tell Aunt Lena she's got a winner."

"Great. Now, are you going to go for it? The reward?" It wasn't hard to hear the hint of excitement in Ed's voice.

I sucked air in between my teeth. *Couldn't I just be a cupcake taster?* "I think so." I placed my hand on his forearm. "Don't you dare tell Corrigan."

He pretended to zip his lips. "Not a word. Speaking of the gallant detective, I better go so he can make time with you."

"Bye, Ed. I'll call you." Rather than turn around, he raised his arm and gave me a backward wave.

I scarcely had time to gobble down the rest of the cupcake and wish for more when I heard Corrigan's footsteps. I swung my door wide open, and as soon as he stepped inside I greeted him with a full-on lips parted kiss. He responded in kind then pulled back.

"I like your enthusiasm, but is it just to distract me?" He wiped some frosting from the corner of my mouth.

"What do you mean?"

He squinted. "Ed. He was a man on a mission. Usually

that mission involves you getting into trouble."

"It was nothing. My aunt wanted me to taste a new cupcake." I had no intention of discussing the reward for Eileen's killer. In my experience, diversion works best. I placed my hands flat on his chest. "If you'd rather I not be affectionate…"

He pulled me back into his arms and we moved toward the sofa. We could start there. Unfortunately, we ended there too when my phone rang. It was my father.

I hadn't heard from him since we'd had a spirited discussion about me working for Gino. He was for it. I was against it. Although I'd kissed him good-bye that evening, we weren't exactly thrilled with each other. Needless to say, I had to answer his call or look like an immature brat.

"Claire, you busy?"

I glanced at Corrigan, who was tucking his shirt in. "Just a little."

It was as if he hadn't heard. "Gino told me about you finding Eileen. Are you all right?"

"Yes, Dad. Remember, I handled murder cases before I turned into a filing goddess again." Sarcasm coated my words.

He ignored my childish tone. "I know that, but, well, I still wanted to make sure. Hey, how about you come over tonight? Suzy's trying out a new dish. There'll be plenty. Come on." I could picture him running his hand through his thick black hair. Even middle-aged, the only gray he had was at his temples.

"Brian's here with me." I protested mildly. Then felt guilty. "I'll ask him." My eyes pleaded with Corrigan to decline. He shrugged, refusing to be the bad guy.

I tucked a strand of my dark hair behind my ear and suppressed a sigh. "We'll be there in about half an hour."

On the way over to Dad's, I asked Corrigan about Eileen's dog. I felt sorry for the helpless pup. Even more, I needed a way to introduce the subject of the murder.

Corrigan stared out his car's windshield. "Animal Protective League took him." He shook his head. "Poor mutt whimpered all the way out the door."

I realized I'd made a mistake asking about the dog. I'm such a softie about animals. I hated knowing how sad Eileen's pet was. "Isn't there somebody to take him? Someone besides her brother, Timothy? I mean, maybe there was someone else in her life. Somebody she wasn't getting along with. Somebody who—"

Scowling, he shifted in his seat. "Are you asking because you're concerned about the dog or because you're thinking of getting involved in the case?"

I tried to keep from sounding defensive. "I'm just asking about the dog."

We pulled into my father's driveway and Corrigan shut off the ignition. "And you don't know anything about the reward."

Embarrassed that I'd been so transparent, I hustled out of the car and onto my father's porch. Corrigan followed and seemed about to say something more when my father answered the door, a wide, almost giddy smile on his face. He'd never been that happy to see me.

Suzy was drying her hands on a towel and joined in as my father ushered us inside. She brushed her long, blondish hair away from her face, gave me a big hug and kissed my cheek. Something major was up with these two. I refused to guess what it could be, though.

We had no sooner gotten into the dining room when my father pulled out a bottle of Prosecco and poured the sparkling wine into glasses.

He cleared his throat. "We have an announcement to make." He passed out the glasses and then raised his. "To Suzy, a wonderful woman who's made me a happy man. Suzy and me are engaged."

My hand gripped the glass tighter and I told myself to blink. I liked Suzy, and this wasn't a total surprise, but her relationship with my dad had moved so quickly. It seemed as if one day he was introducing her as the new neighbor who wore too much makeup and clothes a size too small and the next, she was my future stepmother. I didn't begrudge my father happiness. He'd been so lonely after my mom died, with only my aunt and me as company. For a moment though, unreasonable as it seemed, I felt left out. Alone.

I sneaked a glance at Corrigan to get his reaction. He was smiling with that dimple and those perfect white teeth of his looking genuinely happy for them. Ashamed, I became an adult again and banished my feeling of being deserted. I loved my father enough to wish him and Suzy well. I just hoped they wouldn't ask me to be flower girl.

Before Corrigan could take a sip of the wine, his phone rang. Standing close by, I heard almost every word the caller said. My mouth felt dry enough to think my glass had been filled with sand.

When the call ended, he shook his head regretfully, "I wish I could continue celebrating with you, but duty calls. Claire, I've got to go."

It was an effort to get the words out, and I couldn't look at him. "Don't worry about me." I couldn't let on I'd heard what was said. I needed to process the information.

Corrigan gave me a funny look, then shook Dad's hand and hugged Suzy. "Congratulations to both of you."

As soon as he walked out the door, I sank into a dining room chair, feeling like a fallen soufflé.

My father pulled up a chair next to mine. His voice was gentle, like when, as a little girl, I had a fever. "Claire, you're not upset with us getting married, are you?"

"No, Dad. It's that I heard Brian's conversation. He was called to Vincenza Amato's house. A murder." I couldn't bear to say anything about my other realization. It was too gruesome.

My father's face paled and he put his arms around me. "Honey, maybe it wasn't her."

Suzy asked, "Who's Vincenza Amato?"

Already mourning, I responded, "She babysat me. I adored her."

Chapter Three

I couldn't keep my attention on what my father was saying. It was as if his lips were moving, but nothing was coming out. My thoughts were too loud. I knew Mrs. Amato was dead, killed. But by whom? A long-time widow, friendly with all the neighbors, I couldn't believe she had enemies. It had to be a robbery gone wrong. This area of town was changing and maybe not for the better.

My dad must have realized I wasn't listening. "What would you like to do, Claire?"

I didn't have to think. "I want to go to see her." My face burned with shame for all the times I passed her house while she was living. Never stopping to say hello. "I know the police are probably still there, but maybe I can help. Maybe I can—"

Dad interjected, "You'll be in the way. Stay here. We'll have some dinner. Then talk to Brian. Go to the funeral. There wasn't any family left, you know. Bobby died in a car accident and her husband, well, who knows where he is."

Staring down at my hands, I said nothing. Suzy disappeared into the kitchen and returned, holding a glass of chocolate mousse. She handed it to me. "Here. Eat."

With barely a half-smile on my face, I took it and managed a bite. Even the luxurious dessert couldn't get past my constricted throat.

I poured myself another glass of Prosecco and downed it just as Corrigan knocked on the door and stepped inside. His voice was somber. "I came back to see if you needed a ride home."

I'm sorry to say I let my anger come out toward him. My voice was snippy. "I told you not to worry about it."

"Well, don't bite my head off."

"Sorry. Was the victim you went to see Vincenza Amato?" My voice little more than a whisper.

"Did you know her?"

My voice broke and my words garbled. "She was my babysitter. I adored her." I rubbed away a tear that had escaped from my eye.

He sighed. "Oh, God. I'm sorry, Claire." His eyes narrowed. "You're not thinking of getting involved in this murder too, are you?"

I couldn't answer for fear my voice would break and tears would fall. My dad and Suzy stayed near, silently keeping vigil over my grief. Corrigan sat across from me, leaning forward and holding my hands in his. Though, it was the only contact between us, it comforted me.

I didn't say it but I was determined to find her killer myself. It was the least I could do for a woman who nurtured and loved me almost as much as my mother.

I blew out a big breath, hoping to put an end to my inertia. I pushed aside my remorse over what I hadn't done while Mrs. Amato was alive. I'd do what I could for her now.

I gently slid my hands from between Corrigan's. "Dad, I'm sorry, but could we do your celebration another day? This Saturday? I just can't tonight."

Suzy answered. "Of course, Claire. It seems wrong to celebrate right now anyway. Right, Frankie?"

He quickly nodded. "Saturday is good. Why don't we go out to Lucci's? I'll invite Lena and Ed too. We'll call you with the time."

I managed a slight smile. "Good. Thanks."

As soon as Corrigan and I got into his car, I began. "Are there any suspects?"

He pulled out of the driveway. "We'll talk about it when I get you home. Okay?"

Knowing toothpicks under his nails wouldn't get anything out of him, I agreed.

Chapter Four

We rode to my house in silence, but my thoughts were bouncing off each other so hard it was surprising he didn't hear crashing noises. I hadn't mentioned it to my father, but I knew the only way Corrigan would be pulled into another homicide within 48 hours of his other assignment was if the two were related. My stomach churned and I felt nauseated thinking about Mrs. Amato's last moments.

Once we were in my apartment, Corrigan asked for some water. I suspected he was stalling for time, but I got it for him. After he gulped it down, he motioned for me to have a seat.

He lowered himself onto the sofa next to me and patted his knees with the palms of his hands. He brushed his blond hair back from his forehead and released an audible sigh. "Okay. This is what I can tell you. A neighbor found her. Seems the vic—Mrs. Amato was making cupcakes for the neighbor's kid when somebody got to her. We didn't see any forced entry, so it was probably someone she knew."

I tried to process what he was telling me, but a question kept breaking through. "Why would someone kill her? She was a wonderful person. She was baking for a child!"

"Nothing was taken as far as we could tell. Have no idea. But we'll find out. We're canvassing the neighborhood. If anyone saw anything, we'll know about it."

"I'm going to help find the killer. They deserve to be punished." I steeled myself for Corrigan's reaction, expecting him to blow up. When he didn't, I turned toward him.

His mouth twisted, as if he was fighting the words that demanded to come out. At last, he gave in and said, "Claire, I don't think you should." I started to protest, but he put up his hand. "Hear me out. Remember Eileen O'Donnell?"

Now it was my turn to put up my hand. "I know. Mrs. Amato was killed the same way as Eileen." I shivered, in spite of the room's warm temperature.

He nodded. "So you see why you have to stay out of this investigation. This guy, or woman, has killed twice that we know of. Then tied a ribbon around their neck. He or she is a real wacko."

My nails dug into my palms. "All the more reason for me to use my skills in finding this creep."

Corrigan put his arm around me. "Skills? Claire, those other times, you got lucky."

"Lucky? I'm the one who figured out who killed

Constance." My voice rose and I pushed him away. "And discovered Larry's killer. Not the police. Me."

"Okay, but that doesn't mean you should get involved in this one. With a serial killer, all bets are off. Look, I love you, and I'd go crazy if something happened to you. Understand?"

"Yes, but don't denigrate my skills just to try and keep me safe."

He leaned forward, elbows on knees and head in hand. "You're right. But just stay away from this one. Now, I've got to get back."

It was only eight thirty when he left, but I put on my pajamas, made myself some hot chocolate, wishing I had one of my aunt's new strawberry cupcakes, and plopped in front of the television. I didn't want to think about anything at the moment. Unfortunately, that wasn't what was in store for me.

A knock came before I even got through the opening credits for a show. "Open up, Claire. It's me, Aunt Lena."

I thought about pretending not to be home, but she'd no doubt heard the television. I set my cup down and struggled to get off the sofa.

When I opened the door, she was loaded down with a tray of frosted cupcakes, chocolate, vanilla, red velvet and carrot. But no strawberry. "After tonight's news, I thought you could use some fortification."

I tried to smile, but I'm sure it came across as some weird mouth squiggle. "It's hard to believe something so awful happened."

She set the tray on the table and helped herself to one of the red velvet ones. "I'm not surprised, though. Living alone is rough."

It's not so bad. I eyed the chocolate cupcake with chocolate frosting. "But nobody deserves that." I grabbed it before my aunt ate that cupcake too.

She snorted, "I'm sure he considers himself lucky."

"Huh? Are we talking about the same thing?"

"Sure. Your father and that woman's engagement."

I let go of the cupcake. "No! Mrs. Amato was killed tonight."

Her jaw dropped. "Vincenza Amato? You're kidding?"

I shook my head and blinked back tears.

My aunt threw her arms around me. "Oh, Claire! I didn't know. I'm so sorry. She was such a good woman."

Extracting myself from her embrace, I told my aunt what I knew, minus the ribbon angle. "She doesn't have family that I know of."

"Sure she does. A niece, Franny. Used to live in Chicago, now she's over in Beachwood." She reached for another cupcake.

Would there be any cupcakes left?

She peeled the paper off the cupcake. "Life is so unsure. I hope they get the guy who did it and string him up."

I waited a moment, then, "Are you that upset about Dad marrying Suzy?"

She huffed. “I can’t help it. She’s not a bad person, but she’s got too much…ooh la la about her. I’m not sure Frank can handle that.”

“She’s good for Dad. Really. He’s so happy with her and she takes care of him.” I remembered my first reaction to the news and cringed inside. “We should be happy for both of them. They’re lucky to have found each other. Like you and Ed.”

“So you’re not upset he’s getting married?”

“No. not at all.” God for sure would forgive me that little fib. “You shouldn’t be either. He welcomed Ed into the family. Be happy for them.”

She patted my knee. “Okay then. I’ll try, but I’m gonna keep an eye on her.” She hoisted herself from my sofa with a grunt. “You need to get a better couch. This one has had it. Keep the cupcakes and I’ll see you tomorrow afternoon at *Cannoli’s.* And I’m really sorry about Vincenza.”

“I know.” We hugged good-bye and I went to bed.

Not that I slept. No, I turned from one side to the other, never able to relax. My stomach clenched each time I envisioned Mrs. Amato’s body looking just as I’d discovered Eileen. Something had to be done to stop those murders from happening again.

Chapter Five

The next morning, I made a solid plan to catch Mrs. Amato's killer. It was while I was making a cup of tea in the office kitchen. As soon as Gino came in, which was usually around ten, I was going to tell him I needed to pick up some chocolate for a sick friend. I didn't relish lying to him, but I didn't want him to know my real plan, which was finding the Smalley's Chocolates where Eileen had worked. It wasn't just the reward I was after, although if I could claim it without Gino, I'd have enough to start my own business. Even greater, finding Eileen's killer would solve Mrs. Amato's murder too. That's what I believed, anyway.

After I paid a visit to Smalley's to ask if Eileen had any regular male customers, I'd check these men out. The cops had probably done that already, or planned to. But I might be able to get some information they missed. It was a place to start, anyway.

Gino came in around nine thirty, early for him. He was wearing a sports jacket, and not one of the bright plaid numbers he'd picked up in Florida either. His bushy mustache was neatly trimmed and his hair full of gel so it would behave.

"I'm going with Timothy to make funeral arrangements for Eileen."

"Have they released the body?"

"Tomorrow."

"You're a good friend, Gino. I'm sure Timothy appreciates it."

He shrugged. "Couldn't turn a pal down. Besides," he glanced around. "It's not like we're real busy here."

"That's true. That's why I know you won't mind that I have an errand to run while you're gone." At the last minute I decided to be vague rather than lie. Vagueness isn't a sin.

His left eyebrow rose. "Oh? What's the errand?"

I tried to meet his eyes, but looked away at the last second. "I need to pick up some chocolate for—"

He held up his hands to stop me. "Don't tell me for a sick friend. I'm not as dumb as you think. Smalley's has a reward for Eileen's killer."

I lowered my head and stared at my shoes. "Oh, well, I..."

"I'm not mad. If you believe you can outsmart me, go after the reward yourself. I think, though, we'd do better as a team than as competitors. Plus, if we catch the killer it'd be great publicity for the business. I'd even be able to give you that raise you keep asking for."

I felt trapped, sure that by agreeing to join forces, I'd be forced to do all the hard work. But turning Gino down might be a mistake. My response was a cowardly, "Can I let you know later?" I probably should have told him this was personal. But that would mean revealing that a serial killer was at work. I didn't want to tell him the same monster that killed Eileen murdered Mrs. Amato. Not yet, anyway. It was too fresh, too painful to discuss.

"Sure. But don't take too long. I may get the guy who offed Eileen myself and keep the whole reward."

Somehow I doubted that, but nodded. "Understood." I grabbed my car keys and headed out for the Smalley's on Madison in Lakewood, a suburb just west of Cleveland. It was, location-wise, the most likely store for Eileen's job.

As luck, my luck anyway, would have it a busload of senior citizens had just arrived at Smalley's. They crowded around the chocolate cases, oohing and aahing over the confections behind the glass. I couldn't get near any of the employees to question. After ten tortuous minutes, the group made their selections and, giggling over their purchases, loaded back onto the bus.

I managed to secure the attention of a relieved-looking employee, "That was a whirlwind of women."

The middle-aged clerk adjusted her paper cap. Her name tag indicated she was Assistant Manager Becky. She smiled. "Yes, it was. Can I help you?" She donned a fresh pair of clear plastic gloves and prepared to grab some chocolates for me.

My voice was low and somber. "Could you tell me if Eileen O'Donnell worked here?"

She pressed her lips together for a moment. “I couldn’t say.”

I pulled myself up to my full height. “I’m Claire, a friend of her brother, Timothy, and a private investigator. So, you can’t, or you won’t say?”

Becky glanced from side to side, as if making sure nobody could hear our conversation. “I’ve already talked to the police.” She stepped from behind the counter toward the candy displays in the back of the store.

I followed her and picked up a box of chocolate-covered peanut butter cookies, imagining the number of calories I’d consume eating the entire box. “I understand. I’m just wondering if you had any regular customers Eileen waited on.”

“I already told the police there’s only one gentleman like that. He and Eileen used to joke a lot. He comes in once or twice a week to buy chocolate covered pretzels. All I know is his name is Jerry.”

“Does he pay in cash or credit card?” I could get more information on him with a credit card receipt. Of course, that was if she let me see it.

She snickered. “He buys maybe three pieces at a time. Besides, he’s—wait! He just walked in.”

I turned around to see a man walking so slowly I would be a year older by the time he reached the candy counter. His white hair was nothing more than a rim around his head and his glasses were at least bifocals. I doubted he could even tie a bow, let alone strangle anybody. Still, I had to verify. “That’s Jerry?”

She nodded and hurried back behind the counter, leaving me alone, holding the bag of chocolate enrobed peanut butter cookies.

Feeling frustrated and refusing to leave empty handed, I bought the box of peanut butter cookies. No sense in this visit being a total waste.

I was just backing out of Smalley's parking lot when Jerry shuffled out of the store and was picked up by someone in a dark blue sedan with a blue-and-pink Smalley's Chocolates sticker on the bumper. A snail could have beaten him.

Heading back to the office I plotted my next move. When I parked, though, all thoughts of what to do were brushed aside. Corrigan was waiting for me and he didn't look happy.

He approached my open car door. "Okay, Claire. I thought I made it clear you were to stay out of the O'Donnell investigation."

My choices were to slam the door in his face and peel out of the lot or declare my innocence. "I haven't done anything."

He folded his arms. "No? Then what are you doing with a Smalley's bag?"

I tore open the bag and pulled out one of the chocolate pieces of scrumptiousness. I bit into it with relish. My mouth full, "Yum. I had a taste for these babies. Want one?"

He tilted his head toward the sky. "The manager called and told me you were there asking questions."

Caught. Before I could formulate a proclamation of innocence, he added, “I’ve got to go do my job. I’m sure Gino would like you to do yours.” He turned on his heels, thought better of it and turned back toward me. He kissed me hard. “If you behave, there’ll be more of that.”

I smirked. “If I don’t behave, there’ll probably be even more.”

He laughed, got back into his car, and left me standing alone in the office’s parking lot.

Gino still hadn’t come in. I put my purse and the chocolate into my desk drawer, all the while formulating my next step. So far, I’d come out with a zero on suspects for Eileen’s murder, so I figured it might be easier to investigate Mrs. Amato’s life. Unless, of course, I went in on this with Gino and Timothy turned out to be well-versed on his sister’s social life. Somehow I doubted that.

I grabbed another chocolate-covered peanut butter cookie and headed back out to my car. I’d have to stop for something to drink along the way.

The edges of the neighborhood in which Mrs. Amato had lived weren’t much different from my father’s. The houses were showing their ages, but the lawns were well kept. Except for the beer joints and cut-rate stores popping up all around, the area didn’t look that much different from when I was growing up. But the sense of shabby respectability grew fainter the closer I got to Mrs. Amato’s home.

The first door I knocked on was the neighbor’s

across the street from Mrs. Amato. Her name was Mrs. Tonnato and her son had been two years ahead of me in school. She looked out her front room window and hobbled over to her screen door. She squinted at me as if trying to place my face.

"Mrs. Tonnato. It's Claire. Claire DeNardo. I went to school with Jimmy."

A smile replaced her hesitation and she opened the door. "Claire. It's good to see you. Come in." As soon as I stepped inside she continued, "Did you hear about Vincenza?" She wiped her eyes with a handkerchief she carried in her sleeve. "She was such a good lady. Who would do that?"

"I don't know, but yes, that's why I'm here."

"Are you a cop? You know, they've already been here."

I twisted the truth a bit. "I'm a private investigator, working with the police." Okay, so I stretched the truth as if it were saltwater taffy.

"She meant a lot to so many people."

"That includes me." I swallowed hard. Now was not the time to let tears take over. "Did you know if she spent time with anybody recently?"

Her eyes narrowed. "You mean, like a man?" She twitched her mouth from side to side. "Well, there was that music teacher. I don't know his name or where he was from. He was giving her piano lessons. Can you believe that? Piano lessons at her age."

My senses tuned into what I hoped was the right

channel. "What days did he come?"

She put a wrinkled hand up to her mouth, thinking. "Tuesdays. Yeah, Tuesdays because that's the day Jimmy comes home for pasta. It's about the only time I see him." She pursed her lips. "Don't have boys. Once they're married, they never visit."

Ignoring her advice, I asked, "You mentioned a piano teacher. Do the police know about him?"

"No. I didn't think to tell them. I suppose I should. He didn't look like a murderer, but then, what does a murderer look like?"

Corrigan needed to know about this guy, and I would tell him. Just as soon as I checked him out. "That's true. You can never tell about anyone. Which means, Mrs. Tonnato, don't open your door for anybody you're not absolutely sure about."

She raised her hand and bent it at the wrist. "You sound like Jimmy. He wants me to move out of this neighborhood. Where would I go? To one of those," she made a face, "fancy senior living places?"

"I know. My dad has no intention of leaving the neighborhood either. Look, I better go. Got to get back to work. You take care now. Okay?"

Returning to my car, it took me less than five minutes to find two individuals in the area who offered music lessons; another ten to arrive at the first instructor's place.

It was almost noon when a plump man, looking to be in his mid-forties and dressed in a black cloak that reminded me of Jack the Ripper, exited the store I'd planned on entering. I sprinted toward him, shouting, "Donald Billingham! Wait up!"

He halted, looking as startled as a rabbit spotting a car barreling down on him. "What? What?"

Skidding to a stop, I took in a deep breath and exhaled, "Do you teach piano?"

He smoothed his pencil-thin mustache. "Yes, I do, but I assure you it wasn't necessary to practically give me a heart attack to find that out."

"My apologies for startling you, but I need to know. Do you go out to the pupil's home for lessons?"

He sniffed as if I'd asked him if he wipes his mouth on his sleeve. "Never. Anyone interested in being trained by me must agree to come to my studio. No exceptions." His eyes traveled from my feet to my head. By the pinched look on his face he didn't approve of my black casual slacks and multicolored top.

"That's all I needed to know. Thank you for your time." I turned to leave, but spun around again for one more question. "Oh, do you know of any other piano teachers who do go to the pupil's home?"

He straightened the edges of his cloak. "There's Todd Shotswell. Although the man has no business calling himself a pianist. Of course, he plays other instruments. Equally as bad. Now if you'll excuse me I have business with which to attend."

"You've been very helpful. Thank you."

He harrumphed and went on his way.

As for me, Todd Shotswell was next on my list to visit. Unfortunately, his store was locked tightly and the 'Closed' sign turned to face the public. Mr. Shotswell was nowhere in sight.

My plan was to return to his store at the end of my workday at Gino's and before going to *Cannoli's.* Once I met Shotswell I'd decide if he was a suspect. Then I'd have to present this music instructor as a suspect to Corrigan without him accusing me of getting involved in the serial murders. Even though he'd be right. But, since Corrigan didn't answer his phone, I had more time to decide how to go about it.

Back at work, I noticed Gino and Timothy were in Gino's office, talking in hushed tones. Wanting to ask Timothy if Eileen took piano lessons, I knocked on the door.

"Come on in, Claire."

Gino and Timothy sat across from each other. A half-empty bottle of whiskey and two shot glasses sat between them.

Gino, his words somewhat fuzzy, explained, "Needed to unwind."

Timothy was slouched so far down in his chair I wasn't sure he was even conscious. Then he blinked and gave me a drunken smile, his eyes half-closed.

"Can you give Timothy a ride home, Claire? He's in no condition to drive." Neither was Gino.

Wondering if I'd have to then come back and take Gino to his home to sleep it off, I swallowed a sharp retort. “Sure.” With luck Timothy would stay awake long enough to tell me if Eileen took piano lessons.

Gino stood and swayed ever-so-slightly. “Come on buddy. Let’s get you to the lady’s car.”

Timothy was barely able to give me directions to his apartment without dozing off. We managed, though. He lived in one of the older buildings on Detroit Road. Of course there was no elevator. One look at him told me he’d never make it up the stairs without assistance. Cursing Gino under my breath, I got out of my car and assisted Timothy into a close approximation of a standing position.

It was a struggle but I got him up the stairs and in front of his apartment. Thank heaven he didn’t live higher than the second floor. I was huffing from the exertion and could feel the dampness in my armpits. “Timothy, give me your key. I’ll open the door for you and get you inside, okay?”

His hand missed his pocket the first time, but he finally managed to pull his key out and hand it to me. I held him up with one hand and unlocked the door with the other. We stumbled inside just as my phone rang.

Dragging Timothy toward his sofa, I pushed him down onto it and pulled my phone out. Corrigan was returning my call. Breathing hard, I answered, “Hello?”

“You sound out of breath. Were you running?”

“No, I was moving something heavy.”

Timothy chose that moment to moan. Loudly.

“What was that?”

"Nothing. I called you earlier to tell—"

Timothy, seemingly unaware I was there, stood up and unzipped his pants.

I panicked. "Stop it. Keep your pants on!"

"Who are you talking to?" Corrigan sounded none too pleased.

"Oh, crap."

Timothy toppled over, his upper body on the sofa, his legs on the floor. He was out cold. "It doesn't matter. He passed out."

Corrigan sounded angry and a little wounded. "You wanted to tell me you're with another guy who can't keep his pants on? What the hell, Claire?"

"It's not what you think. It's Timothy, Gino's friend. You know, Eileen O'Donnell's brother. Gino got him drunk and then made me drive him home. That's all."

"So that isn't what you called me about?"

"No. Of course not. I called to see if you knew that Mrs. Amato was taking piano lessons from a guy named Todd Shotswell. Maybe Eileen was too."

"So you haven't kept your nose out of these cases. I'm shocked. Truly shocked." Sarcasm dripped from his words.

"Well did you?"

"Got it covered." Papers rattled. "Shotswell has an airtight alibi for Eileen's murder. He was playing clarinet in a concert at Holy Trinity."

Feeling like a kid who's had her balloon burst by a mean kid's pin, I dropped my chin to my chest. "Oh."

"Besides. Eileen O'Donnell didn't appear to have any musical inclinations. There's nothing to tie Shotswell to her. So we still have a big, fat zero for suspects."

His tone lightened. "What time are we getting together tomorrow with the engaged couple?"

With a promise to check and call him back, we ended the conversation.

I made sure Timothy was still breathing and then left for the office to give Gino a piece of my mind. I should have known he wouldn't be in. He must have slipped out shortly after Timothy and I left.

I forced myself to sit at the computer and make a list of everything that both murder victims had in common. It didn't seem to be much. They were both single, late fifties to early sixties. Mrs. Amato was a widow. Eileen never married. Both lived alone in the same part of Cleveland. That was the extent of their similarities. Meaning I'd have to dig deeper.

Before I knew it, the clock said four thirty and it was time to get to *Cannoli's* for my second job. My stomach let out a loud growl and I realized that the chocolate covered peanut butter cookies had been my only meal of the day. My belly was as empty as the promise of leads for this case.

Rush hour traffic in Lakewood isn't much to talk about, so I got to my aunt's bakery only ten minutes late. Still, she was holding a spatula, arms crossed. "Glad you could make it."

"I'm sorry, Aunt Lena. I'll stay and clean up

tonight."

She softened at that. "No need. Just grab an apron." She inspected my face. "You look starved. There's a ham and cheese croissant in the fridge. Eat that before you start to work. I don't want you passing out from hunger." She pointed to a tray loaded with éclairs. "Then bring out that tray. When the cupcakes are done, take that out too."

I practically shoveled the food in, thankful for my aunt's power of observation. Taking a gulp of water to wash it all down, I grabbed the tray of éclairs and slid it onto the shelf in the display case.

Angie, my aunt's long-time best friend and employee, approached me. "Hey, Claire. Glad you're here. This place has been a madhouse all day." She pushed her silver bangs off her forehead with the back of her hand.

A customer rapped on the counter for service. Once he was taken care of, Angie turned to me, "You okay? I heard about your old babysitter."

I sighed, "Yeah. Thanks for asking." Another customer needed attention and while Angie waited on her, I returned to the kitchen.

"Aunt Lena, did you tell Angie about Mrs. Amato?"

Finishing the frosting swirl on the last cupcake, she shook her head. "Angie played bingo last night and found out from one of the other players."

"But it only happened last night. How could anyone have even known?"

She shrugged. "News like that travels fast. And you

know how those women talk." Aunt Lena pointed to the cupcakes. "These remind me. Your father wants us to meet at Lucci's Saturday evening at seven. I told him I'll bring a cake. Lucci's pastry tastes like cardboard."

A flurry of customers the rest of the evening prevented us from any further discussions about my dad or Mrs. Amato.

After washing off the last crumb from the last tray, I kissed my aunt goodnight, waved to Angie, and left. The whole drive home I thought about the people Mrs. Amato played bingo with. Could it have been one of the players holding a grudge? Did Eileen play bingo too? Or was she more of a poker player? A yawn so wide my eyes watered and interrupted my train of thought.

After some sleep, I'd get my thoughts back on track.

Chapter Six

I dragged myself out of bed the next morning, showered and dressed, and had just finished a cup of tea when someone knocked at my door. "Claire, open up. It's me, Brian."

Wondering if this was a social visit or an opportunity to reprimand me for sticking my nose in the two murders, I opened my door.

There was Corrigan holding the pup that had once belonged to Eileen. He clutched the dog tightly as it squirmed in his arms. "I thought maybe you'd like to give this fella a new home."

My jaw dropped. "Oh, sure I felt sorry for him, but—" The puppy took that time to free himself from Corrigan and jump down into my apartment. He quickly circled my legs and pawed at them. When I bent down to scratch him behind his floppy ears, I could have sworn he hummed with contentment.

Corrigan's voice took on a cheerleader quality. "See how much he likes you?"

I straightened to protest. "He's adorable, but I can't

keep him. I'm never home. Plus, my landlady will demand a huge pet fee." The puppy stood on his back paws and leaned against me. When I looked down he gave me those big, puppy-dog eyes, making him irresistible.

"You can't send him back to the shelter." Corrigan looked at me with his big puppy-dog eyes, making him just as irresistible. He coaxed, "What do you want to name him?"

I tsk'd, feeling my resolve dissolving like Alka-Seltzer in a glass. "He doesn't have a name yet?" At that point the pup released a soft whine. I looked to the ceiling. "I don't know why I'm doing this, but okay. His name is Charlie." The newly named dog barked once and wagged his tail.

Corrigan grinned. "In that case, I have a present for you and Charlie." From the hallway he dragged a twenty pound bag of dog food into my kitchen, then pulled out a chew toy from his pocket. "Got one more thing. Be back in a second." He took off before I could say a word. Meanwhile, Charlie and I stared at each other.

When Corrigan returned, he was carrying a cage big enough for Charlie to move around in. "He's cage trained, or so I've been told. Of course, now that you have a new addition to your family, you'll want to spend lots of time with him."

My eyes narrowed. It all came together. The puppy was to take up any time I wasn't at work. "So I won't have a chance to work on Mrs. Amato's murder case?"

A slow flush appeared on his neck, a true sign he knew he'd been caught. Still, he denied it. Then, "I've got to get back to work." He gave me a quick kiss and disappeared as fast as my paycheck on rent day.

After Corrigan's departure, Charlie looked expectantly at me. I merely shrugged. Then had an idea. "Charlie, how would you like to go to work with me?" I don't know if he was a career-minded dog or not, but his stubby tail wagged and that was good enough for me. To my relief, he went without a fuss into his cage. I grabbed the chew toy and off we went. Uncle Gino had a new employee.

When we arrived at the office, I found a bowl for water and set it inside the cage. I didn't trust Charlie to wander around yet.

Gino probably wouldn't get into the office for another hour, so I went back to work on my list of similarities and differences in the lives of the two victims.

I hadn't gotten far when a woman wobbled into the office on spiked heels. Her dress was wrinkled enough to look as if she'd spent the night on a bar stool. Her brown eyes were bloodshot and her auburn hair, a bad dye job, stuck out every which way.

"Can I help you?"

Her voice was that combination of too many cigarettes over too many years and washed down by too much alcohol. "Yeah, I'm looking for Gino. He own this place?"

Where was Gino when I needed him? I kept my voice businesslike. “Yes he does. He’s not in at the moment, though.”

She snorted, “Figured. He was just about three sheets to the wind when I met up with him.”

This was getting a bit much. “Um, if you’d like, I can give him a message for you.”

She plopped down on the nearest chair. “Needed to take a load off. Don’t have anywhere else to go.”

I took a deep breath. “I’m sure you’ll be more comfortable in the waiting room.”

She shrugged. “Long as there’s no way for him to get in and out without me seeing him.”

I assured her the front door was the only entrance and offered her some coffee. She looked like she could use it.

As the beverage was brewing, my mind ran wild with ideas of what Gino had done yesterday after leaving the office. Before my imagination could get too far, though, I shut it down. Some things I just didn’t want to picture.

By the time I brought her the coffee, she had opened the cage door and Charlie was sitting on her lap. “Hope you don’t mind. The little guy wasn’t too happy locked up.” The smile she bestowed upon Charlie softened her whole face.

“That’s okay, but let me know if he gets to be too much.”

Blessedly, Gino chose that moment to stroll into the

office. "Betty!" For one of the few times I can remember, Gino was at a loss for words. "Uh, um, I didn't expect to see you so soon."

Charlie jumped from Betty's lap just as she stood. "I guess the booze makes the memory slip, huh? You promised me you'd help find my sister, Rose. Remember?"

Charlie barked and Gino looked down as if he'd just noticed the dog. He asked Betty, "You brought your dog with you?" He was clearly not a fan.

I couldn't let her take the rap for Charlie. "No, he's mine. Isn't he cute?" Charlie, rather than making it easy, proceeded to growl at Gino. I scooped the mutt up and put him back in his cage.

Gino's nostrils flared. "Claire, dogs don't belong here. Our work is serious. We save people's lives." He was laying it on thick. *For Betty's benefit?*

"I know. This was an emergency, though."

Betty, not to be ignored, jumped in. "Leave her alone. Dogs are good for people. Relaxes them."

It didn't seem to be working on Gino.

Betty continued, "Now are you gonna help me find Rose like you promised, or not?" Her words were tough, but she looked somehow vulnerable, as if she were going to cry.

Gino was a lot of things, but cruel wasn't one of them. He grasped her hammy upper arms. "Sure. Sure I am. Don't worry, Betty. We'll find her."

Dabbing at her made-up eyes, Betty gave him a

wavy smile. “Thanks. I knew you were a stand-up kind of guy.”

Gino returned her smile with his uncertain one. “Claire will take all your info down. As soon as she puts Spot there back in his cage. Or does he need to go outside?”

Apparently, Charlie knew that word, ‘outside,’ and let out an excited bark. I would be getting some exercise today.

When we returned, Charlie happily went into his cage to nap. Gino had retired to his office, probably engaged in the same activity.

It wasn’t difficult to get what I needed from Betty. Rose had been missing for eight days. Betty had already filed a missing persons report, but since her sister was intermittently homeless, the police didn’t seem to be pursuing the case very hard.

Betty gave me a photo of Rose, probably taken in happier times. She’d had a husband, but he was killed in a hit-and-run. Since then, Rose preferred her own company. As far as Betty knew, the last place she’d been seen was walking out of a women’s shelter run by the Catholic Center.

We’d just finished when Gino came out of his office. I didn’t know if he was going to ask for a fee from Betty or not. Either way, he could handle that end of the business. I left them alone and returned to the computer to search for any further information on Rose Grisaldi.

Less than thirty minutes later, Gino announced he

and Betty were going to breakfast. Actually, he put it as, "I'm taking a client out for a breakfast meeting." That meant he planned on taking a deduction for it.

Charlie woke from his nap and whined. He was probably hungry. I'd forgotten his puppy food and understood it was a bad precedent to feed a dog people food. With that in mind, I found a cheese Danish left over from the beginning of the week and we split it. Charlie seemed to enjoy it more than me.

By the time Gino returned from his meeting, it was almost quitting time for me. I couldn't resist, "Did you have a nice breakfast?" Sugar dripped from my words.

All I got in return was "Um hmm." Then, "Did you dig up anything on her sister?" So much for Gino working the case.

"Just the usual 'last seens.' No one has spotted her since last week. But then she didn't exactly carry on a nine-to-five kind of life."

"True. I'll check with my connections and see what I can dig up." He dropped into his chair, massaging his temples. *Too many bellini's?* He paused for a moment. "Given any more thought to combining forces for the reward on Eileen's killer?"

He caught me by surprise. "I…I haven't had a chance to think about it. The dog, here…"

"I'll give you until Monday. I'm gonna go into my office and close my eyes for a while. My sinuses are killing me today."

Yeah, too much alcohol is murder on sinuses.

Once Gino shut his office door, I called Ed. He seemed to always know somebody who knew something.

"Hey, kiddo. You calling about tomorrow night at Lucci's?"

"What?" My father's engagement event slipped my mind. "Oh, no. You're going, aren't you?"

"Wouldn't miss it. Frank and Suzy make a great couple, even if Lena's having a tough time accepting it. You're taking it better than my wife, aren't you?"

"It was a shock, but they make each other happy and that's what counts."

"Yeah, maybe you and Corrigan will be next." His tone was only half-joking.

"Don't place any bets on it." Actually, I had no idea where our relationship was headed. Right now, that suited me fine. "The real reason I called was to find out if you knew a woman, Rose Grisaldi or her sister, Betty. Rose was an on-again, off-again guest of the Catholic shelter."

He repeated Rose's name a couple of times as if searching his database memory. "Can't say I have, but that doesn't mean I don't know someone who does. Why? What's she done?"

I explained, ending with, "The police have probably talked to the shelter's management, but it doesn't hurt to talk to other people. Sometimes you find something different."

"Send me her picture."

"I'll text it to you. If you find anything let me

know." While Ed was putting out his feelers for anything on Rose, I planned to visit the women's shelter. But what to do with Charlie?

I rapped on Gino's office door and opened it. To my surprise, he was actually working on Rose's file. "Gino, could you make sure Charlie's okay? It would be useful to visit the shelter where Rose was last seen."

Straightening the collar on his shirt, he cleared his voice. "I was just going to pay a call to the shelter myself. After you finish the filing and whatever else you have, why don't you and Rover take the rest of the day off? Start the weekend early."

"It's Charlie and, okay, if you're sure."

"Yeah. I did promise Betty I'd do it."

Before leaving to go to my evening job at *Cannoli's*, I took Charlie home and did my best to dog-proof my place. After walking my pup, I even promised him when I got home, we'd sit and watch a movie and share a bowl of popcorn.

I'd just arrived at the bakery and was tying my apron on when Ed found me. "Hey kiddo, this look like the missing Ms. Rose?" He pulled out his phone and showed me a fuzzy photo of a woman who could have been Rose standing next to a guy playing a piano in a lounge.

"Hard to tell, but it could be. Where and when was the picture taken?"

"It's a bar, Sessions, over on West 25th. The guy who took it says it was some time the end of last week. He couldn't remember exactly what day."

"Thanks, Ed. I'll tell Gino. He can pay a visit there."

He frowned. "Tell me I'm not doing this for him."

"No, I asked you for me. I felt sorry for her sister, Betty. I really don't know if Gino will find anything. The police haven't."

He crossed his arms. "Okay then. Gotta go remind Lena why she married me."

"Huh?"

"Ya know, help her, kiss her. That sort of stuff."

"Is it a chore already?"

He waved his hand. "No. Just the opposite. I'm a lucky man. I do this hoping she thinks she's a lucky woman." He turned and headed into the eating area, whistling.

Picking up a tray of cheesecake slices, I wondered how Ed got so smart about relationships.

I had no time to talk after that. We had so many customers that evening, the time went quickly. I had every intention of calling Gino to tell him about Sessions, but all I accomplished was leaving him a message.

Charlie was so excited to see me, he leaked a bit before he got outside. I forgave him, though. It had been an eventful day. For both of us. To celebrate, we watched that movie on television and ate popcorn as I'd promised.

Chapter Seven

Charlie was sleeping in my lap on the sofa when I awoke. We both answered nature's call and had breakfast. I was showering when Corrigan called to find out what time to pick me up for my father's celebration at Lucci's. But I was able to call him back and we set it up.

Getting hold of Gino wasn't as successful. I tried again to no avail and finally chalked it up to him sleeping in. It *was* Saturday, after all.

Before going to *Cannoli's* to work, I decided to visit Sessions. It wasn't my case and I wasn't getting paid for it, but something told me Rose wasn't just a missing person.

Sessions had a crowd even though it was only ten in the morning. The piano that had been in the picture sat in the corner of the barroom and was unaccompanied. I headed toward the bar when it occurred to me since becoming a PI, I'd had more conversations with bartenders than I'd had in all my previous life. This particular one's name was Al. At least that's what his name tag said.

I introduced myself and showed him the picture Ed had given me at *Cannoli's*. Al frowned. "Yeah, she comes here once in a while. Wants to sing all the time. She's not bad if she's partway sober." He handed me back the photo. "Don't recognize the guy. Our regular player comes in at 6:00. You can ask him."

"Do you remember the last time she was here?"

He let out a breath. "Sometime last week. Dragged a customer, John, to the piano to take her picture beside it. You know, this place gets rowdy at night, but she was over the top."

"Was the man in the photo already at the piano?"

"Yeah. If I remember right, they were singing together. After John took the picture and showed it to her, she quieted down."

"Did she leave with the piano guy or the guy who took her picture?"

"I didn't see her or the guy at the piano leave, but John was still here with some friends. They stayed until closing."

I ended with my usual, "Have the police been by to talk to you about this?"

He poured a beer for a customer before he answered me. "Nope. Nobody's been here."

I pursed my lips in disgust. Cops probably figured she was a homeless drunk. Higher priorities.

I thanked him and started toward my car, intent on talking to Gino. Even if I had to visit him in person.

Before I could punch in his number, he finally called me back. His voice was unsteady, but not as if he'd been drinking. Nonetheless, I started telling him what I'd found out about Rose.

His words stopped me cold. "Tell it to the cops. Specifically your boyfriend, Corrigan. They found Rose. Under a pile of leaves in the Metropark."

A wormy feeling crept into my belly. "Corrigan has the case? Are you sure?"

"His partner broke the news to Betty about an hour ago. I'm here with her now."

I dropped the phone from my ear. If Corrigan got this case, Rose had been killed by the same person as Mrs. Amato and Eileen. It felt as if somebody dropped me in a bucket of ice. I shook my head to thaw my mind. Even if I hadn't had a special relationship with Mrs. Amato, I couldn't let this one go. How many more would die before he was caught?

Holding the phone up to my ear again, I murmured, "Give Betty my condolences." Before Gino could say anything more, I ended the call. My next destination was the police station.

Corrigan beat me to the punch by contacting me. "Claire, I'm sorry but I won't be able to make it to Lucci's tonight. Something came up." He sounded beyond exhausted. No doubt the discovery of a third corpse meant more pressure on him.

Without knowing if I was about to make things worse for him or not, I insisted on seeing him in person.

This was the second case in which a piano showed up. Maybe it was a coincidence, but sometimes criminals are caught because of coincidences.

He sighed, "Yeah, okay. I'll be at the station in about an hour."

That would give me enough time to check on Charlie. I frowned. One more soul to worry about. I had to admit, though; the pup had taken up residence in my heart.

All was well at my apartment and I departed for the police station with the belief that pet owning wasn't as hard as I thought it to be.

Corrigan was sitting at his desk. His tie was askew and his normally pressed shirt looked like Charlie had slept on it. He greeted me in a subdued tone, as if he was conserving his energy for the long days ahead.

Not wanting to waste any time, I started right in, telling him about Betty's appearance in Gino's office. Unable to help myself, I said, "Maybe if the cops had spent more time looking for Rose Grisaldi, Mrs. Amato might still be alive."

That pesky vein in his temple throbbed. "If you're here to tell me what a crap job the police are doing with this, stand in line."

I was instantly ashamed. Nothing like slamming a guy's face into the wall to make him feel worse. "I'm sorry. Really, I am."

He shrugged. "What you're saying is nothing compared to the Captain's comments." He snorted, "He calls it encouragement."

If we weren't surrounded by fifteen other cops and assorted criminals, I would have given him a supportive hug. My words had to do. "This is a tough case and you're working hard."

With no expression on his face, he asked, "Is that why you're here? To tell me that?"

"No. Actually I have information about Rose. Maybe even a photo of the guy who killed her." I pulled out my phone and showed him. A spark came back into his eyes and I recounted the story the bartender had told me.

"Don't take this as approval for your snooping into this case," his voice took on the quality of a strict disciplinarian, "but I'm glad as hell you found something. It's the best lead we've had."

Forwarding the picture to him took a second, but I used that time to nonchalantly ask him if he considered the piano to be a recurring theme in the murders.

He leaned toward me, as if ready to take me into his confidence. "No." Before I could challenge him on it, he added, "Not until now." He placed his hand over mine. "Thank you, Claire." He picked up his coffee cup. "Want something to drink?"

"No thanks. And you're welcome." I waited a second. "Aren't you going to warn me away from this case again? Tell me it's too dangerous?"

He rubbed his hand over his face. "If I thought it'd do any good, I would. Just too tired to go against that brick wall."

It made things easier for me this way, but I felt as if I'd kicked an already beaten man. "I don't want to be a brick wall. More a chain link fence. You know, some things get through."

"Sure. Now, I'm going to get some coffee and get back on this case."

That was my clue to vacate the station. "I'll miss you tonight."

His smile was weary, but warm. "Me too."

Outside the station, I was determined to do what I could to solve this crime. Not only for Mrs. Amato and Betty, but also for Corrigan. I'll admit, though, that $10,000 reward wasn't exactly a deterrent.

I returned home to be greeted by my landlady, Molly. Her arms were crossed and she had a scowl. "Hear you got a dog."

My face felt hot, as if I'd been caught in a compromising position. "Yes, just yesterday. I haven't had time to—" Charlie chose then to whimper loud enough to be heard down the hall.

"Claire, you've been a good tenant, but rules are rules. You should've let me know immediately you were thinking of getting a dog. Now that he's here, per your contract, you need to pay a pet deposit, plus a penalty for not reporting it. I'm sorry, but that's a total of $200."

The sinking feeling I had was my body falling into debt. "When do I have to pay it?"

Molly glanced around. "Let's talk about this inside."

Once he saw me, Charlie was so excited he wiggled

and jumped and grunted happy noises. Afraid he'd wet the floor in front of my landlady, I kept him in the cage.

Molly bent down and stuck her fingers between the metal to scratch Charlie. "He's adorable." She stood. "I'll give you until noon, Monday. If I don't get it by then, it's cause for eviction. Per your contract."

"I understand." Maybe my father could loan me the money. If not, maybe the local Humane Society could put Charlie and me up.

After Molly left and Charlie and I attended to his needs, I pulled out my laptop and added Rose to the list of victims. Next came what each had in common. Two out of the three had some piano connection. The police could explore that for now. Next on my strategy was to find out who ran the bingo Mrs. Amato attended. I still didn't know if Eileen played. Maybe Betty knew if Rose did.

Unfortunately, my plan would have to wait. It was getting late and I needed to get ready for dinner with the family. As it was, my arrival was fifteen minutes after everyone else's.

A smile for everyone at the small round table. "Sorry I'm late. Charlie takes up more of my time than I thought he would."

I plopped down on one of the two empty chairs next to my father. Suzy was on his right side. Across from me was my aunt, whose expression reminded me of a string purse, all pinched and tightly bound.

Whoever the genius was who sat my aunt next to

Suzy should have been executed. This was turning out to be akin to putting oil next to water and expecting the two to mix well. As the evening went on, perhaps the comparison should have been putting a match to kindling. It was bound to flare up.

After a round of pleasantries and the server taking my drink order, my dad looked at the empty chair where Corrigan would have sat. "Who's Charlie? You haven't stopping seeing Brian, have you?" He might as well have asked if I'd lost my mind.

Aunt Lena answered for me as if I wasn't there. "Charlie's her new dog. Brian and her are still together. She knows she's got a decent man." Staring at Suzy she went on, "Not too flashy, like some people."

Suzy's eyes turned to slits but her voice stayed even. "Compared to whom?"

My head turned from one woman to the other, sort of like being a spectator at a tennis match.

Ed, next to Aunt Lena placed his hand firmly on her forearm. "I don't think she's thinking of anyone in particular, are you, Lena?"

Biting her lip hard enough to turn it white, Aunt Lena agreed. "Nobody. Just making a comment."

My dad picked up the conversation, looking like a driver trying to avoid smashing into an already existing two-car pile-up. "So what kind of dog is Charlie? Where'd you get him?"

"He's part boxer and some other things. Brian brought him over for me." I wasn't going to explain the circumstances under which I first encountered the puppy. "Speaking of Brian. He really wanted to be here, but he's working a hot case tonight."

Aunt Lena again. "Raising a puppy takes a lot of energy. But you're young and up to it. Other females like an old dog. One broken in by another woman."

Suzy threw her napkin on the table and lifted slightly from her seat. "That's it! If you think—"

Dad's hand on her shoulder stopped her. Then he turned toward Aunt Lena, his bushy black-and-gray eyebrows lowered. As a kid I knew that was the time to make myself scarce. His voice rumbled, "Lena, Suzy has done everything she can to be accepted by you. Even gone above and beyond. I loved your sister, but she's been gone a long time." He turned in his chair to Suzy and took her hands. "I'm marrying a fine woman and I'm lucky to have her."

Suzy gazed lovingly at my father and I couldn't help but be frustrated with my aunt's refusal to accept this. Even after she'd said she'd try.

The ensuing silence at our table was made even more pronounced by the clink of dishes and silverware. Unable to stand it anymore, I broke the hush around us. "Dad, would you like to see pictures of your new grandson?"

My father's face registered a fleeting look of surprise until he remembered about Charlie. "Sure. Or does anyone have an objection to the dog as a new member of the family?"

My aunt, tight-lipped, sat straight in her chair. Ed asked to see the pictures too.

After giving over my phone with the photos of my new puppy, I asked my aunt to accompany me to the ladies' room.

"Why? Do I look like I have to go?"

"Just come."

We'd barely made it through the restroom door when she said, "I know. I've been terrible to that woman. I just can't help feeling Frank's forgotten Theresa."

I put my arms around her. "Have you forgotten Uncle Tommy?"

She pulled back. "Of course not! I love Ed, but he'll never be Tommy…" Though her voice trailed off, she wasn't done. "But Ed is a good solid man. Suzy, she's, she's—"

"In love with my dad. And he is with her. You can see it if you let yourself. Trust me, even though she doesn't look, act, or dress like you'd like her to, she's a sweet, caring person. And if you keep this up, you'll lose my dad. For the sake of the family, be kind. End of lecture."

My aunt said nothing, but I hoped the wheels in her brain were spinning in the direction they needed to keep the peace in the family.

When we returned, silence fell around the table. Aunt Lena sat down slowly, took a gulp of her wine and cleared her throat. "Suzy, Frank, I'm sorry." She took another sip.

Dad started to say something, but Suzy stopped him. "Lena, that's the nicest thing anyone has ever said to me." She raised her wine glass. "To all of us here. May we grow in love and support of each other."

"Hear, hear." My aunt's voice was the loudest of us all.

Dinner proceeded as well as a family slightly tattered at the edges could hope for. As we were saying our goodbyes, Suzy hugged me and whispered, "Thank you." When we separated, she gave me a smile that helped me realize she would, indeed, be a great stepmother.

Yawning all the way home, I wasn't looking forward to taking Charlie outside a final time. That, in turn, reminded me I needed to come up with $200 by noon Monday. Maybe Gino could advance me the money. I chortled. How long would I have to work without salary to pay him back? Aunt Lena would be a better choice to ask, though I hated to do so. She'd freely give me the money, but then bring up me working for her full time again. That $10,000 reward for Eileen's killer was looking better and better. Too bad the killer behind these murders was appearing more and more frightening.

Chapter Eight

Sunday morning I attended mass at Sacred Heart, the Catholic Church that sponsored the bingo Mrs. Amato attended. After the service, the announcements included the next bingo night, Tuesday evening at seven thirty. I planned to be there to see who showed up. Could the piano man in Rose's photo also be a bingo player?

After church, my next destination was Timothy's. Even though Gino, as well as the police, had most likely pumped him for the facts about Eileen's life, sometimes a woman's touch is the key to unlocking more information.

Timothy took so long to answer my knock I almost left.

"Hey, it's you." He opened his door wide and waved me inside. His apartment looked as disheveled as he did. Papers and other trash were strewn about and an empty pizza box balanced on top of a can of beer. Needless to say, the place had a stale aroma. He did too. I doubted he'd bathed since we'd last seen each other.

"Sorry about the place." He rubbed the stubble on his chin. "Can I get you something? A beer maybe?"

"No, nothing, thanks. I just came by to ask you some questions. Is that okay with you?"

"Yeah, sure. I can't think of anything I haven't told Gino and the cops. But shoot." Shoving papers off the sofa he said, "Here. Sit down."

I perched on the edge of the cushion. "Do you know if Eileen ever played bingo?"

He puffed out his cheeks and then blew out the air. "Couldn't say. She didn't mind a good poker game, but bingo? She never mentioned it."

"Okay. Did she play a musical instrument?"

"Cops asked me about that too. I told them she played the piano when we were kids, but she quit right after high school."

A tiny spark of excitement flickered in me. "Did she ever talk about starting up again?"

"Sometimes when she was tipsy she'd mention it. That's as far as it got, though."

"Did she ever say if she'd taken lessons?"

"No." He shrugged. "I don't get it. What do bingo and the piano have to do with Eileen's murder?" He dropped his head in his hands.

I wanted to place my hand on his shoulder to offer some comfort. Instead I sat there like a mannequin, worried it would be misconstrued. After a moment, he looked up. "Sorry. I know you're just trying to help find the bastard who did this."

A knock stopped him from saying any more. It was Gino. Upon seeing me there his lips curled into a wise-to-the-world smile. "Hey Timothy, I see you already have company."

I felt as if I'd been walking around with the back of my dress tucked into my underwear. Knowing my information gathering was at an end, I wanted to make a quick exit. "Hello, Gino. Timothy and I were just winding up our visit. I'll see you at the office tomorrow."

Gino's smile didn't fade. "Yeah. I'll be in early."

Once inside my car, I reassured myself Gino wasn't angry, just surprised I'd shown so much initiative. At least now my similarities list could include the fact that all three victims either played piano, wanted to play, or was last seen by a piano. Not much of a tie-in but better than none. Wondering if the police had found the piano player from Sessions, I called Corrigan. Maybe he'd tell me in exchange for…for what? He probably already knew Eileen was a former pianist. He'd just be mad I was still on the case.

I quickly ended the call. Too late. He called me back. "Hi Claire." He sounded more cheerful than the last time we talked.

"Hi Brian. What's new?" I grimaced over the lameness of my question.

"We brought in a person of interest."

My breath caught. "That's great." A vision of the $10,000 reward disintegrating into dust flashed before me. "Is it the piano guy from Sessions?"

"Yep. He'd been buying her drinks all night and left with her."

A glimmer of hope danced in front of my eyes. "But you don't have anything to tie him to Mrs. Amato's or Eileen's murder."

His voice tightened. "Let's not discuss this over the phone."

"You brought it up."

"Yeah, well. I shouldn't have." He dropped the brusqueness. "I have some hours off. I'm going to get some sleep and then you want to grab some dinner with me?"

"Sure. What time?"

"I'll call you when I wake up."

He may have felt better with this person of interest. Seeing too many loose ends, I was as unsettled as a mouse in a lion's den.

The rest of my day was somewhat productive. I stopped at my dad's to explain my situation with Charlie and my landlady. He didn't even wait for me to ask for the money. He even offered to bring a $200 check to Molly the next morning. A rush of gratitude warmed me. It didn't last long because then he dropped a bomb on me. He and Suzy planned to sell both their houses. Start fresh. It was understandable. Still, I hated the thought of someone else living in the house that had been my home and I didn't want it to happen. My smile was no doubt stiff, but I assured him the idea was a good one.

Afterwards, I felt proud for not letting on how I felt

while simultaneously criticizing myself for being so childish. A melancholy sigh escaped. Time stands still for no one, including me.

I was feeding Charlie when Corrigan texted me. He'd be over at seven and we'd have dinner at the West Ender.

He met me at the door as I was bringing Charlie in from his walk. The dog seemed to remember Corrigan and tried to hide behind my legs.

Corrigan laughed and in a coaxing voice said, "It's okay. I won't take you away, Charlie." Eventually the dog allowed Corrigan to pet him and even to escort him to his cage.

My plan had been to be cool about the person of interest, but I couldn't help myself. Even before we reached his car, I was asking Corrigan about the murders. "What makes you think this guy is the killer of all three women?"

He opened my car door. "He was the last one seen with Rose and he has no alibi for the times of the other murders. Plus, he has a history of assault. Charged twice but neither stuck."

Waiting until he got inside the car, I responded, "That doesn't mean he did it, though."

We pulled out of the parking lot. "Unless something happens to make me think otherwise, he looks good for the murders."

Could the police be squeezing this guy into the mold just to solve the case? Telling myself not to start an argument, I changed the subject and recounted dinner at Lucci's.

At the restaurant, we were getting along fine until I finished my first chocolate martini. Leaning into Corrigan, a challenge in my voice, I asked, "So tell me. How did this guy know Mrs. Amato and Eileen? There was no forced entry in either case. Or have you decided that wasn't important?"

"I was wondering when you'd get back to that." He carefully wiped his mouth. "Okay, Claire. We haven't figured that one out. But we will. Now look. I'd like to have a pleasant dinner with you. Otherwise I would've grabbed a burger and slept until it was time to be back at work."

Pressing my lips together, I vowed to keep my doubts to myself. "Sorry, but I think the killer is still out there." Great. I broke my vow faster than a monk watching a striptease.

He closed his eyes and it was obvious he was trying to stay calm. "Noted. Maybe he only killed Rose. That bit about the red bows around the victims' necks is being kept under wraps so the media doesn't run with a serial killer angle. But maybe someone leaked the information. Who knows?"

Covering his hand with mine, I said, "I'm sorry. Let's have a nice dinner together." His half-smile told me he agreed, but wasn't quite sure it was possible.

Dinner and dessert finished, we returned to my apartment. Multiple kisses later, we were horizontal and

I, for one, was very glad we'd dropped the murder conversation. From the response of Corrigan's body, I'd say he was too.

Unfortunately, a cop during an investigation is always on duty. His phone rang, dousing our mutual passion. He growled, but still answered. When he hung up, he was once again no-nonsense Police Detective Brian Corrigan. His cheeks puffed out and a breath escaped. "Rick Gutkowski, our person of interest, disappeared. Slipped right through our surveillance." He put on his shoes and grabbed his car keys. "Still think he's innocent?"

Running away certainly didn't help the guy's case any. "Okay, so maybe he's guilty of something. Just not all three murders."

Corrigan snorted. Then, with a quick, preoccupied kiss, he left.

Chapter Nine

In my pre-Charlie days, I normally showered, ate breakfast and headed out for the office, all in silent slow motion. That Monday morning, Charlie and I trudged outside to take care of his needs. Back in the apartment, he wanted some attention and ran in a circle around me. Then he rolled onto his back. I rubbed his puppy belly, marveling at how trusting he was. I stopped once he settled down. I toasted a Pop-Tart for my morning meal. The aroma got Charlie excited again. As an ardent admirer of the pastry, he finally sat motionless at my feet. Sucker that I am, I shared some of it with him and flicked on the television.

My quick breakfast turned to cement in my stomach. A reporter, wearing that 'this is tragic, folks' look was describing a murder that occurred Sunday night. He called the perpetrator of this fourth victim the 'Red Bow Killer.'

Unlike the other bodies, this latest corpse was found in the suburb of Brook Park, south of the other murder locations.

Having the media grab onto this story had to be Corrigan's worst nightmare. A panicked city and increased pressure from the politicians to charge someone with the crime was beyond bad.

Unbelievably, it got worse. The reporter went on to claim the police had questioned someone of interest, but had let the suspect slip through their hands. He concluded by asking anyone with information to notify the police. I felt ill, with a buzzing in my ears. All the police needed now was a bunch of wanna-be detectives looking for the suspect. It'd be like hunting someone hiding out among fun house mirrors. Lots of sightings, no real results.

That's when I realized my phone was vibrating. "Claire!" It was Gino, who no doubt had also seen the news. "You better be on your way to the office. We have some serious work to do."

Sure he meant I had some serious work to do, I countered with, "What exactly will *we* be doing?"

As if he were the lead of an espionage ring, he lowered his voice. "Our mission is to find Rick Gutkowski."

I shook my head, picturing Gino with his hand over the phone, as if anybody was interested in eavesdropping on him.

By the time I stepped into the office, Gino had both computers up and was talking to Betty on the phone. When his call finally ended, he looked as if he'd donated blood but they mistakenly took all of it. "Whew! She's needing some serious hand-holding. Guess I'm the man she chose to do it."

No reply that didn't include sarcasm came to my mind.

I looked down at my phone. A text from Ed had come in a couple of minutes ago. He was downstairs, waiting to talk to me. Alone.

Rushing out the door, I told Gino I needed to get something from my car. Ed was in his security guard uniform so I assumed we didn't have much time. After a quick greeting he told me why he'd come.

"That hotel where the latest was killed? Somebody was having a party there and Lena did their cake. Afterwards, she went over to pick up the dish and stuff because the customer didn't return it. Body had already been found. Anyway, victim's name is Desiree Luscious."

My eyes narrowed. "What? What kind of name is that?"

"Stripper or exotic dancer. Take your pick. Real name is Joanna Whitechapel. Worked at a place called Diamond Girls. I thought you'd want to know."

That was the extent of his information, but it was a start. After thanking him he saluted me and took off.

Heading back to the office, I debated whether to let Gino in on this or not. I half-smiled. No doubt he'd love to have to visit a strip joint for an investigation. I decided not to tell him. Not yet. The thought of having that

$10,000 reward all to myself was just too enticing.

"Did you get what you needed?" Gino asked as soon as I returned.

"Huh? Oh, yeah. Did Betty have any more information?"

He rubbed his chin. "Nah, but I got the latest victim's name. Get this; Desiree Luscious." He smirked. "Found out where she worked too. I think I'll pay a visit there and see, I mean find out what I can."

My jaw clenched. It didn't seem like there'd be any way for me to keep ahead of Gino. I forced myself to get philosophical about it. Maybe it wasn't so bad. After all, he had more years of experience in investigations than me. I waited a moment. Nope, I wasn't buying it.

Gino had his keys in his hand and was ready to visit Diamond Girls when a man the size of a Kodiac bear pushed past me. The stranger torpedoed toward Gino, grabbed him by the collar and tossed him back into his chair as if dropping a handball. His voice was rough and low. "Keep your hands off Betty. This is your only warning." He spun around, growled at me, and exited.

I rushed to Gino and leaned over. "Are you okay?"

He blew out a shaky breath. "Think so." He righted his shirt which still showed the creases where the stranger had bunched it.

"Who was that?"

Gino wiped the sweat off his forehead with his handkerchief. "Probably the guy Betty told me about, Clarence. But she claimed it was over between them."

I straightened up. "Didn't look like anyone told *him*."

He rubbed his neck and rocked his head from side to side.

"Do you want some water or something?" He declined. "I hate to interfere with lovers' spats, but maybe you need to talk to Betty and have her straighten Clarence out. Like now."

"I was going to go to Di—"

"Tut, tut, tut." I wagged my index finger back and forth. "You need to do it now. I can go to…" I feigned ignorance. "What's the name of the place again?"

He hung his head, disappointed no doubt. "You're right. Just be careful. Place is Diamond Girls. Maybe call your dad and see if he'll go with you."

I glared at Gino. "I'm not five and afraid of crossing the street by myself." It was one of the few things I wasn't afraid of.

I waited to leave until Gino called Betty and asked her to meet him at the office.

***

Diamond Girls was on busy Brook Park Road, in an area of industrial parks. The sign outside claimed the joint was newly remodeled and under new ownership. It still looked dingy to me. Once inside the place, it looked like all the rhinestones in the world had been rounded up and glued to the walls. The glare must have been awful. The carpet was a swirl of red and black, probably to hide any unseemly stains. The stage was in the middle of the room and a pole sat off to one side. An enthusiastic young woman gyrated clumsily for the benefit of three bored-looking men.

One of the men stood. "That's fine, honey. We'll call you."

Honey pouted and climbed off the stage.

At the back of the showroom was a hallway with some doors. Maybe that was where the dancers got ready. I started heading that way when one of the two guys still sitting spotted me and, with his elbow, poked the third man. All three of them turned in my direction.

The standing guy spoke first, "You here for tryouts?"

I halted and half-laughed. "No, no, I'm not."

The third guy snorted. "Good thing. You ain't got enough to hang pasties on."

The first guy protested. "Hey, with surgery she'd be all right. You ever think of having a boob job, honey? I know a doc—"

This was already out of control and I hadn't even asked a question. I raised my voice, "Excuse me. I'm not here about a job." *Although I bet I could work those tassels.* "I'm with Francini Investigations. I have some questions about Desiree Luscious." The third guy finally stood. "I'm Tony Esposito, the owner of this place. We already talked to the cops." His consonants were blunted, as if he was from Chicago.

My pat answer was in-the-ready. "I understand. We work with the police to make sure nothing's been omitted."

Tony expectorated into a plastic cup just as I finished my spiel. "Yeah, well, they didn't miss nothing. And we're busy here."

"This'll only take a minute. Did she have any regular customers?"

The first guy at the table chuckled, "None of the guys here are regular people."

Tony frowned. "Don't mind him. Thinks he's a comedian. To answer your question, no. Although all our girls are required to mingle, you know."

I kept my face neutral, all the while imagining watered-down drinks for the girls and illegal extra-curricular activities.

"But surely, somebody saw something last night—"

"Nobody seen nothing. Now, if that's all, we got a business to run. Nick will show you to the door." Tony puffed out his chest like a snake before it strikes. "If you don't want any trouble, don't come back."

The guy I supposed was Nick hiked his pants over his protruding belly and moved to take my arm. I yanked it out of his reach. "I don't need any help." I spun on my heel and hoped to make it beyond the door before my trembling knees gave out.

Outside I blew out a big breath. *That went well.*

I'd just reached my car when a woman got out of a truck and started walking toward Diamond Girls. With her white-blonde long hair, unnaturally large breasts, super-high heels, and pants so tight blood cells would've had to move single file down her legs, she had to be a dancer.

"Wait! Miss!" I called but she didn't turn around. Desperate, I shouted, "Did you know Desiree?"

The woman picked up her pace. "I don't talk to reporters or cops." Her voice was high, almost squeaky, like the sexpots in movies.

"I'm neither. Just a friend of another victim."

She halted so quickly I thought she'd fall backwards. "Ooh, in that case, okay. Hey, I'm sorry about Desiree. She was a doll. And clean. No drugs. Mingled, but that's all she did, if you know what I mean. Always left after her shift. Claimed she had another job as a hostess, but I don't know where." She looked toward the building and flinched. "Gotta go. Nick's coming."

Sure enough, Nick, shoulders hunched was barreling toward us.

With a quick thanks, I leaped into my car and gunned the motor.

After making my getaway, I headed back to the office. I needed more background information on Desiree to see the connection between her and the other victims. So far, if there was a pattern to the women the killer chose, I didn't see it. Maybe it had something to do with her other job. I just had to find out what that job was.

Betty and Gino were sitting at his desk and were so deep in conversation when I returned they didn't even notice me. That was fine; it would give me time to do some research. Too bad I only got as far as Desiree's last residence before Gino called to me.

"So what'd you find out?"

"Ms. Whitechapel was a 'good girl.'" I made quotation marks with my fingers. "At least according to one of the other dancers."

He frowned. "Nothing else?"

"The owner is a guy named Tony Esposito." I also described Nick.

Gino sighed, as if I was a student who couldn't rise above a C+. "Shoulda trained you better on interrogation techniques."

My hands curled into fists, but I said nothing, telling myself I'd find the killer, get the reward, and be out of this office before Gino could ask if I'd made the coffee yet.

Betty interrupted. "I need to take off. Meeting with the funeral home." She covered her mouth with a waded tissue. A sob still escaped.

I gave Gino a nod, as if to tell him to go with her. He jutted his jaw in defiance, but in a voice that could soothe a lobster going into a pot of boiling water, said, "I'll go with you, Betty. You shouldn't have to do this by yourself."

Dropping the tissue from her face, she brightened just a little. "You sure? I mean, thank you. Oh, thank you so much." Up went the tissue to block another sob.

After Gino gave me the order to 'hold down the fort,' he and Betty left. Back I went to research Desiree's life.

It took me about an hour to find all I could. Desiree aka Joanna lived alone in an apartment on Memphis Avenue. No siblings. Parents never married. Mother deceased. Father, whereabouts unknown. Graduated from Garfield Heights High School. Started at Tri-C College but dropped out the first year. Currently employed at Diamond Girls. Well, that was no longer the case. No information on her alleged second job.

I was ready to pack up, but my conscience wouldn't let me leave until Gino either returned or called. While waiting, I made a list of questions about Desiree's life; then a list of questions I still had about the other victims. Once that was done, I drummed my fingers on the desk. Finally, I called Corrigan. Maybe he'd drop some information about Desiree. I chortled to myself. That would happen about the same time chocolate became calorie-free.

Of course his voicemail picked up. The guy was probably going crazy. Four murders and now he'd probably be working with the Brook Park police. I left a message and, since it was almost quitting time, I closed up shop.

Silently thanking Ed for talking Aunt Lena into closing *Cannoli's* on Mondays, I reckoned I had the whole evening free. My first stop was at Rally's for a burger, fries, and diet pop. I justified the calories by telling myself I hadn't had lunch.

Taking the last sip of pop, I pulled into Desiree's apartment complex and drove around. I didn't have to guess which one was her building. There was a black-and-white police car and, of course, Corrigan's car parked outside Building D. No need to wonder what they were doing there.

Swallowing my desire to wait until the police left, I made my way toward the building. A uniformed cop prevented me from getting very far. Stalled, I spotted Corrigan and shouted to him.

He looked to the sky and shook his head. Still he made his way over. "Tell me you're here because you have something to add to the investigation. If not…"

I tried not to look smug. "As a matter of fact, I do. The victim worked at Diamond Girls and—"

He flipped open his notepad. "I know. Her stage name was Desiree Luscious."

"She had another job."

His eyes narrowed. "Where?"

I looked down at my feet and muttered, "Don't know." Then I raised my head. "I'll find out though."

He stifled a yawn. "If you do, make sure the police are the first you tell." Peering out at the parking lot, he blew out a weary breath. "And Claire, don't give the reporters any information, okay?"

I scowled, "As if I would." Turning my head I spotted camera operators and reporters bearing down on us like boll weevils on a cotton field. No way to stop them.

Since I didn't look like anybody important, it was relatively easy for me to slip through the media people.

They descended on Corrigan, though, with a fervor that reminded me of army ants picking a carcass clean. I turned away, unwilling to watch the carnage.

Travelling down the road to uncover Desiree's other job could have been be a waste of time, but I had nothing else. I said a silent prayer to St. Jude, the saint of impossible causes, that the killer would be stopped before he snuffed out another life. A short plea that I'd be the one catching him and so, getting the reward followed. If only I could talk to someone else at Diamond Girls.

It was almost nine when I got my next brilliant idea. "Hello, Ed? It's Claire."

"What's up, buttercup?"

"Just wondering what you're doing tonight."

He chuckled. "Hey, I'm a married man." His tone turned serious. "This about those four murders?"

"Yes." I told him how Tony Esposito had interrupted my questioning the dancer. "So, can you meet me at Diamond Girls and sort of run interference for me?" I was purposely vague because the exact plan hadn't yet come together in my head.

"Lemme get this straight. You want me to go to Diamond Girls and put a hold on this Esposito guy so you can slip in and talk to this other dancer?"

"Something like that."

"That ain't smart, Claire."

I bit my lower lip. "Do you have a better plan?"

"I will by the time I get over there."

I didn't know if he was bluffing or not, but we agreed to meet at Diamond Girls at a quarter to ten.

Chapter Eleven

It seemed as if Charlie and I had both just settled down to sleep, he in his cage and me in my bed, when my alarm went off. Tuesday morning already. I dressed to the local news.

The same serious-looking reporter as the other day held a piece of paper and addressed the television monitor. "We've just learned the police have apprehended the man they believe to be the Red Bow Killer. Now to Kirstie Radner with the latest on this situation."

An attractive, thin brunette wearing glasses flashed onto the television screen. "We're here at an apartment in Ohio City where police, acting on a tip, discovered the man they believe may be the Red Bow Killer. My understanding is, Rick Gutkowski will be charged with the murder of four women in the Cleveland area."

"No!" I yelled at the television screen. I still believed he didn't kill Mrs. Amato or Eileen. Or was it wishful thinking? If he was the murderer, I could kiss the reward goodbye.

I grabbed my purse and headed out the door. I needed to play my hunch and check out all the bingo halls on the West Side. *What could it hurt?*

First, though, I had to make an appearance at the agency.

Gino was already at work when I arrived. "Did you hear they caught the guy who killed Betty's sister, Rose?"

"Yes, I heard. I don't believe it though." The words slipped from my tongue before I could catch them.

"You don't believe they got him, or that he's the killer?"

"Never mind. I'm just talking." I faked a yawn. "Didn't sleep much last night so my brain is a little foggy."

Gino rubbed his chin with his thumb and index finger. "Wish we'd have caught the creep. Wouldn't have minded that reward lining my pocket." He added quickly, "Yours too."

I smirked. "Yeah, plus I bet your value in Betty's eyes would've also gone up."

Leaning his chair back, his head resting against his palms, he sounded wistful. "There's that too." He pulled himself out of the mood. "Well, no use crying over spilt beer. Wishing for a different ending sure ain't gonna pay the bills. Or your salary. What else we got?"

Going through the list of pending cases, I found one that only needed Gino's sign off. I printed the invoice and handed it to him. "Here. If this is okay, sign it and I'll set an appointment with the client for you."

He flipped through the file. "I remember this guy. You hadn't started back here yet. Kind of a strange old guy. Wanted to know if his nephew had anything to do with the kid's own mother's death." Gino chortled. "In my opinion, the nephew should've been investigating the uncle." He took the invoice and signed it.

After making a quick phone call, I said, "The client has agreed to come in today at one this afternoon to make his final payment and receive the report." Without taking a breath, I asked, "Do you mind if I leave the office for a couple hours? I need to check up on my aunt. She wasn't herself last night."

"Sure. Just be back by noon. I want you here before this…" He glanced at the invoice. "…Wolden guy shows up."

"Definitely." To leave and start my hunt for Desiree's bingo place I would've agreed to just about anything. I had to follow every possible lead before I could rest and go along with the conclusion that Rick Gutkowski really killed Mrs. Amato.

Having to hustle, I practically jogged to my car. Not counting church bingo, there were five places on the West Side. One was in Berea, a small city southwest of Cleveland. Three were in Brook Park. Since Desiree lived and worked in the area, the Brook Park bingo halls seemed the places to start.

All three of the Brook Park halls were dead ends. It was nearing noon when I pulled into the Corey Bingo Center in Berea. Pounding on the locked door produced no response. I was just about to go back to my car when the door finally opened. A man in coveralls, about fifty, said, "You didn't have to try to break the door down. I was in the basement."

"Sorry. I'm in kind of a hurry."

"Aren't we all? What can I do for you?"

I introduced myself and then showed him a picture of Desiree. "Did this woman work here?"

He slid his glasses down his nose and peered at the picture. "Joanna. Yeah. Used to be a hostess here but she quit last week." He shook his head. "The wife and I just heard what happened to her. Awful. Just awful. Glad they caught the guy, though."

I didn't want to chit-chat about Desiree's demise and waved his last comments aside. "Do you know why she quit?"

"Something to do with a guy." He raised his hands and shrugged. "Don't know exactly what, but that's the story."

"Is there anyone else here who might know more about it?"

"My wife, Helen, but she's off on an errand. She should be back..." he looked at his watch, "...in about ten minutes if you want to wait."

I rubbed my forehead. Gino would be less than happy if I didn't make it back in time for his client, but this was important. Maybe Helen would return earlier than he expected. "I'll wait a bit."

"No sense standing out here. Come on inside. I'm George, by the way. Me and Helen own this place."

After five minutes, I questioned the wisdom of agreeing to wait. "Thank you for letting me hang around, but I really can't stay—"

A woman's voice interrupted me. "I'm back." Helen spotted me. She placed two white plastic bags on the counter. "Are you here for the hostess job?"

"No, sorry." I introduced myself as a PI working with the police and asked if she could tell me why Joanna quit.

Helen tsk'd and made the Sign of the Cross. "That poor girl. May she rest in peace." She squinted. "But I thought they caught her killer."

"The police have a person of interest. We want to make sure it's an iron-clad case."

"Okay then. Joanna claimed one of the customers was making her nervous. She was pretty sure he was following her home. She wouldn't tell me who it was. Said she didn't want to make any trouble."

That meant Helen couldn't give me a description of the stalker. "Are you or your husband here during the bingo games?"

She shook her head. "No. That's why we have or had a

hostess. Our niece is filling in for now. George and I own another bingo hall in Akron and we're down there most evenings. It's closer to home."

"Have you talked to the police about this guy or what Joanna told you?"

"They caught her killer so quickly I didn't think I needed to."

My phone rang just then. Gino, no doubt wondering where I was. I ignored it. "Do you have a camera videoing the bingo games?" Maybe the stalker guy would be on those videos. I was desperate for a break in this case.

"No. But if you come back tomorrow night, one of our regulars, Louise, used to talk to Joanna. She could maybe describe him to you. We also have bingo on Fridays, Sundays, and Mondays."

"What time does bingo start tomorrow?"

"Seven, so if you get here by six thirty, you can ask Louise questions. After they start calling the bingo numbers, don't even try to get anyone to talk to you."

After thanking George and Helen, I headed back to the office. On the way there, I called Corrigan to tell him what I'd learned. When it went into his voicemail I shook the steering wheel, imagining I had him by the shoulders. It seemed he was never around when it was important for a case. But when I was messing up, he managed to be right there. With no other option, I left a message asking him to call me ASAP.

By the time I pulled into the office parking lot it was almost one thirty. Making my way up the stairs and into the office, I concocted an acceptable excuse. To my surprise, Gino was alone. He looked up at me, his face contorted into a furious scowl. "Where the hell were you?"

Composing my face into what I hoped was sheer

contriteness, I said, "I'm really sorry, but my aunt was in worse condition than I thought. She was so jittery she couldn't even frost cupcakes. I had to do it for her. Then she needed me to fill the cream puffs. I did it as fast as possible. When you called, I was elbow deep in whipped cream." I said a quick prayer hoping I hadn't just jinxed my aunt.

Gino folded his arms across his chest. "Okay, okay. Family comes first. But next time, you call me. I had to handle that crackpot by myself and it wasn't easy."

It was time to reassure Gino. "You must have done a great job and satisfied the guy. He wasn't here long."

"Gotta know how to talk to people, Claire. That's the secret to success."

Suppressing a groan, I asked if he wanted more ready-to-close files.

"Yeah, two if we got 'em."

The rest of the afternoon passed like corn syrup dripping off a spoon. It probably didn't help that I kept checking the time every five minutes. Finally, blessedly, the business day ended.

Having already told Aunt Lena I'd be working late tonight and tomorrow night, I headed back home to feed and walk Charlie and to ring Corrigan again, since the man hadn't returned my call.

Still he didn't pick up, but this time I left an even more detailed message regarding what I'd learned at the bingo center. Maybe that would get him to talk to me.

After shoveling down a Lean Cuisine and savoring two chocolate-frosted brownies, I departed for Sacred Heart's hall for bingo. For me, being lucky tonight meant finding out that the Red Bow Killer wasn't already sitting in jail and I could collect the reward. For Mrs. Amato, who had played bingo at

Sacred Heart's, being lucky meant I'd find her killer.

The church's bingo games weren't scheduled to start for another hour, but you'd never know it by the crowd of people already seated with their cards and markers. I got one bingo card and strolled around the room, pretending to be engrossed in the card's numbers. The majority of players were women, middle-aged and older. The few men there were around the same age as the women they accompanied.

Since the tables were filling up fast, I took a seat at Table 8 in the back. A few minutes later, one of the deacons announced the game was about to begin. Taking another glance around the room, I felt a wave of disappointment. Unless more people came in later, this was going to be a long night with little to show for it.

The first game ended when a frail-looking woman yelled bingo. While the deacon went over her card to make sure she actually had the right numbers, the door opened and a few other players came in. I cringed. One was Angie, my aunt's friend and employee. I could only hope she didn't spot me since I'd lied to my aunt. I slid down into my chair, but it was too late. Angie smiled and headed straight toward me. The other people at my table made room for her and she sat to my right.

"I didn't know you liked bingo." When I gave her a weak smile, one of her overly-plucked eyebrows shot up. "Okay. What are you really doing here?"

"Please don't tell Aunt Lena you saw me." I went on to explain my motives.

Angie looked set to respond when the deacon began calling out the numbers for the second game.

It seemed to last forever, and I was beyond relief when at long last, someone yelled bingo.

Angie nudged me with her bony elbow. "Let's go to the restroom and talk."

Staring into the mirror fixing her bouffant hair, Angie said, "I won't tell Lena if you promise me one thing."

All sorts of demands she could make rushed through my mind. What choice did I have? My aunt would be furious to know I lied to her, never mind that she'd think I was still playing detective and risking my life. Which I was, but she didn't need to know.

"What am I promising?"

Angie grinned. "If you're wrong, and the real killer's already in jail, I won't say anything to Lena. If you're right, I want to help catch this creep." She held up her hand to stop me from protesting. "I know, it could be dangerous, but this guy needs to be caught. Vincenza Amato, was a good woman and if this monster could kill someone like that, what's to say he won't get me next, or you, or even Lena? I want to be able to go home at night and not be crazy with fear that I'm gonna be wearing a red bow the next morning. Now that's the end of this discussion." She took a breath.

"Plus, I know the regulars here and it's none of them. So that saves you time. We need to go to other bingo halls."

I closed my eyes, wanting to turn her down. Angie has been Aunt Lena's best friend since my aunt was eight and Angie was seven. If something happened to Angie, it would devastate my aunt, and she'd never forgive me. At the same time if she knew what I was doing instead of working at *Cannoli's* when she needed me, she'd be furious. My aunt can hold a grudge. She still isn't talking to my cousin, Adriano, because he didn't come to *Cannoli's* grand opening five years ago. "Okay. But you have to do what I say."

She grinned like a human version of the Cheshire Cat.

"Sure."

"All right then." I cleared my throat. "Let's go back and watch for any strangers coming in."

"That's it? That's all we're going to do tonight?"

"PI work isn't as action packed as it is on television."

From the corner of her mouth she said, "I can see that."

By the time bingo night was over, neither of us won a single pot. Or identified possible suspects. One other guy came in after the initial arrivals. He was on oxygen, so he wasn't a likely Red Bow Killer candidate.

Before we exited the hall, I told Angie I would drive her to her car. "Just because we didn't spot the guy doesn't mean he's not around. Once you're inside your car, don't unlock it until you get home." Once she agreed to that rule, I added, "Next time there's a bingo game, don't drive to it alone. Have your son drop you off at the door and pick you up. In fact, he can bring the whole family."

In mock obedience, "Yes, mom."

"I'm serious." Then I told her about attending Corey's Bingo Center the next evening.

She snapped her fingers. "Ooh, I can't go with you. My grandson is playing in a school concert. I've got to be there."

Promising to fill her in on any pertinent happening, I drove her to her Ford and made sure she turned the engine on. The doors automatically locked. She waved as she pulled out of the lot. Sure Angie could no longer see me, I slumped in my seat, relieved she couldn't make it the following evening. Chances were a lot better for spotting the killer, if indeed he was still free, tomorrow night at Corey's. I didn't want to worry about Angie's safety. I'd be too busy worrying about my own.

The lot was pretty empty by now, except for a few cars. I

smiled noticing two of the remaining ones had Smalley's Chocolates bumper stickers. The idea behind those was that if a vehicle was spotted with a sticker the driver won free chocolate and their name up on Smalley's marquee. I hadn't noticed before but a lot of people had the stickers.

Before I pulled out of the lot, I checked my phone. Corrigan still hadn't called. Now I was really annoyed.

Chapter Twelve

It was the next day before Corrigan called back, leaving a message that he'd try again later. Of course, I was indisposed at the time, refusing to take my phone into the ladies' room.

All morning and most of the afternoon, Gino had me go through the files again and jot down what was needed to wrap each up. It was grunt work, but the day went quickly. Before I knew it, it was time for bingo. Again.

The parking lot at Corey's Center was about half full by the time I arrived. Helen greeted me at the door. Rubbing her thumb and index finger repeatedly over a button on her print dress, she asked, "Are the police coming too? In case that man who upset Joanna is here?"

I didn't want her to know the truth, that I was working on my own. "They won't come inside. We wouldn't want to disrupt the game. I'll check out the stalker myself and make sure he's the right guy before anything is done."

Rather than looking at me, Helen's eyes darted around the room. "That's best." She smoothed out her short, steel-gray hair.

"Is Louise here yet?"

"She's at the first table, second chair. Heavy-set woman. Wearing a green top." Helen handed me a bingo card and a marker and whispered, "On the house."

Luckily, nobody was seated on Louise's right side. I sat down next to her and introduced myself. Louise didn't look impressed. "If you and the cops did a better job, Joanna would still be alive. She was such a sweet kid." Her sagging cheeks shook as she made her pronouncement.

"I understand how you feel, but concerned citizens like you can help right the wrongs." I sounded like a public service announcement. "Now, please, what can you tell me about the man who stalked Joanna?"

She leaned toward me. "I stay after sometimes, ya know? Live alone so what's the hurry to get back? Anyway, one night I noticed she's shaking as she's putting stuff away. I asked her what was wrong. She says one of the guys here followed her home. Didn't talk to her or nothing, but, still…That's like stalking. Anyway it scared her. I told her to go to the cops. She didn't want to. Happened one other time and she quit. But they arrested the guy who killed her, so why the interest?"

I should have been prepared for the question, but it took me by surprise. "We want to make sure we have the right man in custody. Now is this stalker guy here?"

She scanned the room. "I don't see him."

"Could you give me a description?"

"Tall, blond hair. Nice-looking. Good build. That's all I remember about him. Sorry."

Disappointed, I still reassured her. "That's okay. If he comes in, you tap my foot with yours. Would you do that for me?"

"Sure." A bell sounded. "Ooh. That's the warning bell to get ready." She lined up her five cards and grabbed her marker, moving her spare in case the one in hand ran dry.

The hostess started things off by explaining house rules, followed by her spinning the small cage next to her. The tiles clacked and bounced around. The entire room seemed to hold a collective breath. She pronounced, "B-2. That's B-2."

The first three spins and picks passed by me. I was too busy looking for…someone who looked like a serial killer, I suppose.

On the fourth spin, she called out, "I-22. That's I-22." I glanced down and realized my card had an I-22. I quickly dotted it. Then came an O-65. That one was on my card as well. In the same row. Despite this being an investigation, my excitement grew and by the time the hostess had called another letter and number on my card, my belly felt like it was fizzing. So great was my concentration, Louise had to kick me twice.

She finally hissed, "I think he's here. By the door."

Not wanting to turn my head and look, I tried to see him from the corner of my eye. No good. Plus I missed the previous number called. It didn't matter. Someone from the next table over yelled bingo and I spun around to face Desiree's possible killer. Our eyes met.

Yep, tall, blond hair, nice-looking. Just as Louise had described him. It was Corrigan.

As he made his way toward my table, Louise's hands began to shake. "He knows we're on to him. Quick, do something!"

"Relax, Louise. He's just—"

"Hello, Ladies. Just what, Claire?" As smooth and cool as gelato, Corrigan pulled a chair over and sat between us.

"I was going to tell Louise that you're a police detective."

Louise's eyes opened wide and her words tumbled out. "I don't know anything. Honest. Anybody could be the stalker. Doesn't have to be you."

Corrigan's eyebrows knit. "Desiree's stalker looked like me?"

"Desiree was Joanna's nickname." I explained to Louise.

"Oh." She paused. "I think so."

"Or did you see me on TV Monday?"

Louise cradled her double chin in her hand. "I don't think…Well…Now that you mention it…"

Much to my annoyance, Corrigan looked smug. Unwilling to let him dismiss my theory again, I brought up Desiree's fear that she was being stalked.

Corrigan nodded. "Duly noted."

Louise excused herself to get different bingo cards.

She lumbered over to the welcome area, leaving Corrigan and me to talk.

"What about bringing Louise down to the station and seeing if she can recognize your suspect."

Corrigan's laugh was short and sharp. "You must be kidding. She's not reliable. Hell, she thought I was the stalker. Good try, though, Claire."

"Why are you here, then?"

"Are you kidding me? All those voicemails you left me." He gave me a Huck Finn-like grin. "I had to get them to stop. So here I am."

I shook my head as if to say he was incorrigible. "Are you going to stay in case the stalker comes here?"

That tasting-soured-milk look came over his face. "Didn't plan to. Tell you what. I'll stay through the next games if the two of us can play our own games afterwards."

Louise returned just in time to overhear Corrigan. Rather than being embarrassed, she sighed, "That takes me back to the last proposition I received. It was quite a while ago, when I was still a looker."

Thankfully, the hostess began calling the numbers and that conversation ended.

As did the evening, with nobody coming into the bingo center after Corrigan. The two times I'd spent at bingo had yielded nothing. I consoled myself, thinking at least tonight I'd get some much appreciated physical attention from Corrigan. Or so I thought, until his phone vibrated. We hadn't even gotten out of the parking lot.

It was hard to tell by the light of the street lamp, but I think his face paled. He mumbled, "Be right there." And I knew.

"Another body? At a bingo hall?"

He stared at his phone. "Body was found in a back parking lot. On Lorain, near Kamm's Corner."

Squeezing his upper arm I said, "I understand. You have to go." Being an adult, I didn't even remind him about my belief Gutkowski wasn't the Red Bow Killer. Being right didn't make me feel any better.

Against my protests, he walked me to my car, barely met my lips with his, and took off. Once he was out of my sight, I pouted. Another night of cuddling with Charlie. Oh well, at least he wouldn't notice if I didn't shave my legs.

Charlie was happy to see me, which cheered me up a bit. We took a quick walk and then, once he realized it wasn't mealtime, he sat on the floor next to me while I booted up my computer. Sure enough, the online news was full of information about this latest victim of the serial killer. Her name hadn't been released yet pending family notification. *Poor Corrigan.* His name was scattered all over the stories. The Cleveland Police Detective who'd caught the wrong guy. Gutkowski was being released and most likely thinking of suing the city.

Grabbing a chocolate chip banana muffin from my freezer, I waited for it to thaw a little before biting into it. Charlie got a doggie treat. Then I returned to my computer. Nothing added up. Eileen didn't play bingo or, as an adult, the piano. Mrs. Amato did both. Rose was near a piano but didn't play bingo. Desiree played bingo. Piano playing was unknown. The only common factor across the board was that they all lived alone. If that was the only thing driving the killer to choose them, a lot of women, including me, were at risk.

A chill cascaded down my body and I shivered. I turned off my computer in favor of the television, telling myself the information on this latest victim would be of enormous help. Sure, and Charlie was really a prince cursed by an evil witch.

After an hour of watching the tube and learning nothing new, I double-checked the deadbolt lock on my door and made sure my windows were sealed tight. Funny how living alone had never seemed quite so scary.

***

Early the next morning, even before showering, I checked to see if there was anything new on the woman murdered the previous night. Unfortunately, it was all just a rehash of old information. After taking care of Charlie and my own needs, I drove to the office.

The first time all week Gino hadn't beaten me here. It wasn't long, though, before he wandered in, looking like he'd been picked up by a tornado and dropped in front of the office. His shirt was buttoned wrong and he'd missed two belt loops. His hair, usually neatly parted on the side, stuck out as if trying to escape from his scalp. "Gino, are you okay?"

He plopped into the closest chair. "Yeah. Spent the

night with Betty. Clarence showed up." He smirked. "Let me just say he won't be back."

Whether or not he wanted me to ask, I didn't want to know any more than that. "How about I make you some coffee?"

"Naw. I've had enough of that stuff. Been up since five." It was now nine thirty. He scratched the back of his neck. "Heard there's been another Red Bow murder. This one near Kamm's Corner, by the West Park library."

"What else have you heard?" If he had known about Desiree before I did, he was a steady user of the police scanner he claimed to have.

He sat back in the chair. "Are we partners in the reward money?"

I let out a deep breath, weighing my options. This case was getting more frightening by the day. Plus, $5,000 was better than nothing. "Yes. Okay. We're partners."

"The victim was on her way home from the library. That was the last place she was seen. Name was Wendy Nichols and she lived on Chatfield. She was a waitress at that pancake house in Rocky River. Figured I'd go to the restaurant. Get breakfast. Ask around."

"That means I get the library?" Figures he'd go for the easier task. He stood and smoothed his shirt with his hands, but the creases were too deep to disappear. "Think I'll take Betty with me."

Sure, another meal he'll write off as a business expense. *Big spender.*

Leaving at the same time, I was convinced of my accomplishing more in one hour than he would all day. I was already regretting my decision to share the reward.

My visit to the library garnered me very little. According to the librarian I spoke with, Ms. Nichols was a regular there. That she usually checked out nonfiction was the extent of what the woman could tell me.

Just outside the building, an elderly lady stopped me. She pushed her thick glasses up with her index finger. "Are you with the police, dear?"

"I'm a private investigator, but I do work with the police." Believing she was just nosey, I prepared to excuse myself.

That is, until she said, "Wendy wasn't killed by that Red Rover Killer, was she?"

"You mean the Red Bow Killer. Yes."

The woman's hand flew to her mouth. "Oh dear!"

"Did you know Wendy well?"

"Sometimes we'd talk. Usually about what book we'd read. Yesterday, I saw her leaving just as I was coming in. She had some books on playing games."

I was on alert now. "Games like bingo?"

"I didn't get a good look at them. The only reason I knew they were games is because the top one had a checkerboard or something like that. I didn't have my glasses on."

"Was there anything else you remember?"

A man followed her out." She pinched her chin. "Or maybe he was just leaving at the same time. I'm not sure."

"Could you describe him?"

"He had one of those oxygen thingies on. I suppose that's not important."

Recalling the bingo player on oxygen, I wondered how many men in this area carried oxygen around with them. I grasped the lady's hand. "Thank you! Thank you!"

I spun around and went back to the librarian, describing the guy and asking if she'd ever seen him.

"Why, yes. He's over in History and Current Events right now. And I believe he's been here before."

Barely letting her finish her sentence, I raced to that section. Nobody was there. I searched the rest of the library to no avail. *How did he get out without me seeing him?*

Finally, I went to the checkout desk, wondering if information on the books someone checked out was confidential. It was.

Amazingly, Corrigan answered his phone. "Hi. Can you come to the West Park library? Right now, so we can see what books Wendy Nichols checked out the night she died."

I could feel his irritation through the phone. "Three books. One was on bingo, one on playing clarinet, and the last on attracting men. None were found with her body. And before you ask, she didn't own a clarinet."

"Yes, but that means bingo is the link."

"You're forgetting Eileen and Rose. Neither played

bingo."

"As far as we know." I was reaching. "Maybe it's bingo *or* music." Turning to the ridiculous I even muttered, "Maybe it's oxygen."

"What? Claire…" A warning in his tone. "Sure. Maybe what gets this guy off is a woman playing the piano and singing out bingo numbers. Who knows? The one thing I'm sure of is that, whoever he is, he's not anything you've run across. Please. Stay out of this."

He was correct, of course. And I was alarmed and worried. This guy's murder streak was the stuff of nightmares. But the lure of even half the reward, plus getting whoever killed Mrs. Amato was too strong. Plus, for me and for all of his potential victims I wanted it all to end.

"You're right, Brian. Look, I better get back to work. Gino's probably wondering about me." I'd skirted his request with a non-answer. It wasn't my best response, but at least no lies were involved.

All the way back to the office I thought about Wendy Nichols and why she was killed. She wasn't at a bingo parlor the night she died. Was it just the idea of bingo that made her a target? Or maybe it wasn't bingo, it was music. Ideas were darting through my brain in no particular order, sort of like bumper cars.

At work, it came as no surprise to me that I'd be alone. Gino hadn't returned from his so-called fact-finding breakfast. My guess was that the only facts he discovered were whether Betty liked pancakes or waffles better.

Actually it was good having my boss gone. It gave me time to look up when the bingo parlors in Brook Park had games. I couldn't risk Aunt Lena's displeasure by calling off one more night, but luckily, St. John's Catholic Church on Bunts Road near Detroit Avenue had bingo tomorrow afternoon at four thirty. I could at least sit in for a couple of games before leaving for *Cannoli's*.

I let Angie know where to meet me and explained I'd have to leave bingo early. She'd be on her own. I wasn't happy about that, but there wasn't much of a choice.

Afterwards, I typed up the last few invoices and opened the mail. Nothing but bills and junk mail. If Gino didn't get some new clients, we'd both be working at *Cannoli's*.

I drummed my fingers on my desk, drank a cup of tea, and decided I'd waited long enough for Gino. Digging through my purse, I found the address of the piano instructor, Todd Shotswell. Corrigan had assured me Shotswell had a solid alibi for Eileen's murder, playing in a concert, but what about for the other murders? Or maybe we hadn't identified all the music teachers in the area. I'd checked Cleveland's West Side and nearby suburbs. But how could I be sure my search had been broad enough? Back to the computer I went, this time to search for musicians outside the immediate area.

There were four of them who gave lessons. The first one's line was disconnected. The second person no longer taught or even played due to a chronic illness. The final two were women.

I shook my head, knowing I was grabbing at a cobweb. You know it's there, but when you snatch the thing it drifts out of reach.

I rubbed my shoulders and rolled my neck. Maybe I just needed some music to soothe me.

Chapter Thirteen

The door to Shotswell's music store and studio was open. Inside it was not exactly dark, but I had to strain to see the man as he set down a clarinet. "Can I help you?"

"Yes." I skirted around a drum set and a guitar. "My name is Claire. I'm wondering if you know of anyone who gives music lessons." If he said he did, my rudimentary plan was to take one and let him know I liked bingo. Then watch his reaction.

He stood and turned on a floor lamp. The man looked to be about forty-five with thinning medium-brown hair and a compact body. "I give lessons in the student's home. Are you asking for yourself?"

"Yes. Yes, I am." I had about as much musical ability as my dog, Charlie.

"And what instrument are you interested in?"

I didn't own a piano so I glanced around for inspiration and found it. "I've always wanted to play saxophone." I swallowed hard, hoping he did the same with my story. He stepped closer to me and brought the sharp, sweet odor of his cologne with him.

I stammered, "Of course, I've…I've never played it before. Or any instrument. I guess you could say I'm musically disadvantaged." I wondered if my dad still had the old sax he used to play when he was young.

Shotswell's laugh was hearty and pleasant. "That's no problem. Most of my students have little or no experience with music. Some of them might even be tone-deaf." Although his comment wasn't kind, his tone was not unkind. "I like to think of my students as 'diamonds in the rough' if that makes any sense." He smiled warmly.

"It does." Despite my suspicions, I found myself genuinely smiling back at him. Still, I came there for information, not to make a friend. "By the way, do you have a card?"

"Yes." He pulled one from his pocket. "I'm Todd Shotswell." He stuck his hand out and shook mine with a solid, strong grip. Then back to business. "If you've never played, I suggest we start with the alto saxophone. It's the easiest for beginners. Now I can rent you one for $20 a month. It's like new."

I told myself I could expense it out. Just like Gino was no doubt doing with his breakfast. "Okay, but can I have my first lesson here? I have a roommate and—"

He held up his hands to reassure me. "Say no more. I don't usually do this, but we can start off with lessons here. After a few weeks, we'll discuss it again."

We talked price and set up a tentative schedule.

Although I tried to get my first lesson the next day, he claimed prior commitments and our session wasn't until next Wednesday. Stymied, I left with a slightly used saxophone and a how-to booklet. My frustration lessened when I decided that if my father still had his saxophone, I'd bring this one back. It'd give me a chance to do what I should have done on this first visit. Talk about bingo.

I stashed the rented instrument in my trunk and returned to the office just as Gino was settling into his desk. "How'd it go, Gino?"

He burped into his hand, and I could detect a hint of breakfast sausage in the air. "The vic was a saint." He waved away the comment. "You know, everybody's a saint when they die." He snorted. "Wendy Nichols was a waitress at the pancake place since 2010. Best friend was another woman named Flo, just like in that television show." He chortled. "Maybe the cook is named Mel." When I didn't laugh he went on. "Flo says she dragged Wendy to St. John's bingo game once, but Wendy wasn't into it."

I stopped him. "Maybe the books were for Flo?"

"What are you talking about?"

I gave him a quick rundown of what books the latest victim had checked out of the library.

Rubbing his chin as if considering my point he said, "Could be. We won't ever know that now. What about you? Uncover anything?"

Showing him Todd's card, I described my plan.

"You gotta be kidding me? Sax lessons? And that's

gonna help you find the killer? We already know this music man had a hell of an alibi for Eileen's murder."

My jaw tightened. "Maybe. Then again, what if music has something to do with these murders? You know it could." I turned the discussion back on him. "Did you find out if Wendy Nichols played an instrument?"

He templed his fingers. "As a matter of fact, she didn't."

"You're sure?"

That's when he admitted he hadn't asked. "I had to get Betty back home." He pulled out a piece of paper. "Got Flo's number, though." He picked up the phone. "And I'm calling her right now."

Sometimes I wondered how Gino had stayed in business for as long as he had. I glanced around at the shabby office décor, a faded blue sofa that had seen better days, chairs that wobbled when you sat, and a picture on the wall that looked like the product of a nighttime art class. All a direct reflection of Gino's PI skills.

Luckily, Flo answered her phone and Gino redeemed himself. "Thanks. You're a sweetheart." He hung up and shook his head. "She played the harp."

"Harp?" Tilting my head to the side, "Then why the book on the clarinet?"

He shrugged. "Don't know. But that's what Flo claimed. So I think we need to put a list together of what each woman had in common."

I blew out a breath. “Already did that.”

“Okay. What did you come up with?”

Looking at the letter opener on my desk, I contemplated stabbing Gino with it rather than explaining once again what I’d already told him.

He rubbed his chin as if he was thinking deep thoughts. “We need to check out all the bingo parlors around here.”

Little did he know how close he was to being seriously injured. Holding my temper, I reviewed my experiences at bingo and ended with my findings of zero. Lucky for him, before going into my future plans, Betty walked through the door. Her mascara had run down her face and she looked like a mask from a Mardi Gras ball.

Gino jumped up. “What’s wrong?”

Betty handed him an envelope. “From Rose, before she…” Her voice trailed off as she swallowed a sob.

He gently guided her to a chair and slipped the envelope from her hand. Inside was a note. Gino skimmed it and his face paled. His voice was as solicitous as a lawyer when explaining a will. “Do you mind if I read this to Claire?”

Betty shook her head.

“Dear Bets, Sorry I disappeared on you again, but I felt too confined. Met a guy (don’t I always?) who likes music as much as me. Piano, guitar, even clarinet, it doesn’t matter. He’s crazy about it all. Says he’s crazy about me and maybe someday it’ll be ‘til death do us part. Be happy for me. Love, Rosie.”

When he finished reading, Betty dropped her head in her hands. Her shoulders shook. "I shoulda took better care of her."

Gino dropped to his knees and tenderly placed his hands over hers. "Claire, get her some water."

Mesmerized with Gino's softness, it took me a moment to move.

When I returned with the cup of water, Betty was wiping her eyes and Gino was talking to her in soft tones. He took the glass and had her take a sip. "Betty, we need to get this note to the cops. After we make a copy for ourselves."

I volunteered to take it to Corrigan. Maybe he'd finally agree I was right in believing that music somehow played a role in these murders.

On my way there, I called my dad to thank him for paying my landlady and to find out if he still had his saxophone and what type it was.

"Yeah, still got the old sax. It's a tenor. Why?"

"I'm, um, taking lessons."

He laughed. "When you were young your mom and I tried to get you to play the flute. You flat out refused. So what's up with lessons now? Especially a saxophone? I know you're not planning to play at my wedding."

Telling him the truth was out of the question. "I just think it'd be fun. You always seemed to enjoy it."

"Yeah, I did. You know, your mother thought it was sexy when I played."

"Dad!" I wrinkled my nose.

He chuckled, "Okay, I'll stop. If you want it, the tenor sax is here for you." His tone turned serious. "Oh, by the way, Lena claims you've been working late with Gino."

I bit my lower lip, fearing my lie would bite me on the rear. "Yes. Was she upset?"

"No, but I've known Gino long enough to know he'd never work extra hours. Tell me you're not using the time you should be at *Cannoli's* trying to find that Red Bow Killer.

"Dad, I—"

He interrupted me and, using his I'm-the-father voice, said, "I'm not done. Now I want justice for Mrs. Amato as much as you do. But not at the risk of losing you. So here's the deal. I won't tell Lena what you've really been up to if you tell me you're done with trying to find this murderer."

My spirits, already low, sunk so far down an expedition would be needed to find them. It was bad enough that this investigation was proving to be terrifying. Now my dad was holding the truth over me. Just like Angie. I wondered if, after all, it wouldn't be better to confess to Aunt Lena and appeal to her mercy. But then that'd implicate Angie and I didn't want my aunt mad at her friend. "You can rest assured, Dad, there's no way I'll be finding the killer."

"I suppose that's the best I'll get from you."

"Love you, Dad. I'm at my destination. Gotta go."

I ended the call before he could say another word.

Feeling like the last kid picked for a dodgeball team, it was me and me alone. Nobody was happy about my investigation except Gino, and that was for personal reasons. Now here I was, in front of the police station to show Corrigan Rose's note. He might not know about my lie to Aunt Lena, but he was just as adamant about me dropping this case as my dad. But then nobody has ever wanted me to pursue an investigation. Everything is fine when it's over and I've solved the murder. Until the next one. Sure, I'm absolutely petrified during it all, but I go on. What would it take for them to accept that I was a competent PI? How many times would I have to prove it to them?

Enough! I threw back my shoulders, held my head high and marched into the police station, Rose's note in hand. After pleading with the cop at the reception cubicle, I was able to locate Corrigan. He was sitting at his desk and motioned for me to come over.

He pointed to the note, his tone lighthearted. "I hope that isn't your resignation from being my main squeeze."

"No. As long as you behave, you won't ever get that."

He gave me a suggestive smile and lowered his voice. "Depends on what you mean by behaving."

"Well, for example, you can tell me what's been going on with the Red Bow Killer."

His good mood evaporated like water in a hot pan. "I thought we discussed your dropping out of this case."

"You're right. We *did* discuss it." I waved the note

in front of him. "But I keep getting dragged into it."

"What do you have there?" He reached for the envelope.

I pulled back. "Not until you tell me something I probably don't know."

He appeared to be considering my request, then, "Okay. I bet you don't know you can be arrested for withholding evidence." He motioned for me to have a seat.

I ignored his gesture. "That wasn't what I meant." I turned toward the door, hoping he wouldn't call my bluff. It'd be tough trying to solve this crime from behind bars.

"All right, Claire. But don't think you're back in this game."

Quickly seating myself I said, "I'm all ears."

He glanced around and then back at me. "We just learned that ten years ago there were twelve murders in Pittsburgh. Same M.O. Police made an arrest but the guy hanged himself in his jail cell before trial. The murders stopped, so the cops figured they had their man."

Listening to the story, I'd clutched the neckline of my blouse so tightly my hand ached. "Have you checked if anyone like, Todd Shotswell, lived in Pittsburgh?"

"I've already told you one thing. But here's another, just to show good faith. No record of his living there. Now hold up your end of the deal." He stuck out his hand.

A deal is a deal, so I explained how the letter came

into my possession and dropped it in his upturned palm.

He read the note twice. The second time around he started chewing on his lower lip. “Betty’s sure this is from her sister?” I nodded. After a moment, “Okay. Thanks for bringing this in.” He stood and put his suit jacket on.

“Wait a minute. Where are you going?”

“To walk you out.”

“Aren’t you going to do anything with the note?”

“You wanted one piece of information. That was the deal.”

Despite bombarding him with questions, he remained closed-mouthed all the way to my car. A quick kiss on the lips and he turned back toward the station.

I leaned against my car, fuming. Why did he have to be so stubborn about me staying out of this?

The drizzle that had started when we walked out of the station turned into a shower, so I jumped into my car and stewed over what Corrigan’s next move would be. Finally, I calmed down enough to recall that the last time I’d seen Timothy he’d had a ragged and stained Pittsburgh Pirates tee-shirt on. A gift from Eileen?

I’d been out of the office for close to two hours and Gino was probably wondering what happened. But before going back, I made a detour to Timothy’s place.

As soon as I parked in front of Timothy’s apartment building, Corrigan pulled up. It seemed like the only luck I’d had recently was bad luck. I sighed. At least the rain had stopped.

Spotting me, Corrigan leaped from his car, shaking his head as though I were a heavy chain around his neck. Once we were within speaking distance he practically spat, "What're you doing here?"

In a voice I hoped sounded like I was immune to his surliness, I responded, "Same as you, I imagine. Finding out if Eileen had ever lived in Pittsburgh."

Once he was beside me, he said, "We'll go in together. I do the talking. Deal?"

"Deal." I went for my next question. "What about the other recent victims? Did any of them have ties to Pittsburgh?"

He blew out a breath, probably wishing he could blow me off. "Police are investigating and before you hound me about it, they're doing the same with Rose's letter."

We didn't talk again until we were right outside Timothy's door. "Remember—"

"I know. You do the talking."

As soon as Timothy opened his door, he hugged me as if I were his best friend. "Claire! I'm so glad you're here. Look around. I cleaned myself and my place up."

Stepping out of the hug, I gave him the biggest smile I could muster. "I'm so glad! It must have been hard though."

He looked down at his feet. "Yeah. It was. But you and Gino have sure helped me."

Corrigan cleared his throat. "Detective Corrigan, Cleveland PD. We spoke before. I have a few more questions regarding your sister."

Timothy's eyes moved from me to Corrigan. "I remember you. Are you helping Claire?"

He might as well have asked Corrigan if he was my serf. While I suppressed a smile, Corrigan's mouth twisted and he firmly set Timothy straight. "No. We happened to arrive at the same time. If you'll just answer my questions I'll be on my way."

"Sure. But I think I've told the police everything I know."

While Corrigan was pulling out his trusty notepad, I offered, "Sometimes something you don't think is important turns out to be what helps solve the case."

Corrigan actually gave me a nod of approval. "Claire's right. Now, did your sister ever live in Pittsburgh?"

Timothy's thick eyebrows bunched together. "Yeah, but that was ten years ago. She only stayed a year or so. Why?"

Pen poised, Corrigan continued, "Do you know if Eileen was involved with anyone while she lived there?"

Timothy squinted and turned to me. "What's this about?" He shifted from one foot to the other.

Softly coaxing Timothy, Corrigan repeated himself, "How much do you know about any relationships your sister had while she was in Pittsburgh?"

Timothy scratched his head, thinking. "Not much at all. She was sorta skittish when she got back. Coulda been over a guy. I didn't ask." He bit down on his lower lip. Then, "Maybe I should have. Why are you bringing this stuff up now?"

I couldn't just stand there. All those women murdered in Pittsburgh while Eileen was there and she's the first victim here? It couldn't be a coincidence. "This is really important, Timothy."

Timothy raised his palms upward. "Why? What does her living in Pittsburgh got to do with her murder or anyone else's?" His expression changed. "Did this same sorta thing happen there?"

I guess I didn't exactly react with a poker face.

Timothy moaned. Then he quickly gave us heated glare. "You think Eileen knew this Pittsburgh murderer?" Spittle appeared in the corners of his mouth. "Maybe they were partners? What kinda stupid theory is that? If you really believed it, why aren't you working with the Pittsburgh cops?"

I tried to backtrack a bit to change the tone of this meeting. "We're just collecting information right now. Nothing more."

Timothy didn't give a verbal response. The look on his face said it all; he didn't believe me.

Corrigan gritted his teeth. I'm sure he wished he'd duct taped my mouth before we knocked on the door. "We *are* working with the Pittsburgh police. But it was ten years ago. People who worked those cases retired, died. Plus, Claire's right. We're looking at your sister's murder from every angle possible to catch this guy. So we're asking a lot of questions."

Every inch of me wanted to spill everything we suspected, but I refrained. "Timothy, believe me. This is just one more avenue we're exploring. We *will* find her killer."

Timothy grabbed my hands into his. "I gotta believe in you, Claire. It's what keeps me going."

"Sir, anything else you can recall when your sister got back from Pittsburgh could help."

Timothy dropped my hands and ran one of his through his hair. He blew out a breath. "Can't think of anything else. Eileen wasn't much of a talker."

"I understand. But if you do think of anything, no matter how small a detail, please let us know." He gave his card to Timothy. "Thank you. We'll be in touch soon." Corrigan had his hand on the door and threw me a look that meant I needed to leave with him.

Corrigan walked me to my car for the second time. "Couldn't let me handle the questions, could you?"

"He asked why we wanted to know." It was a poor excuse, but I didn't have a better one.

To my surprise, Corrigan didn't argue with me or remind me that he was the cop, not me. Instead, in a reflective tone, he said, "The guy seems really attached to you."

Thinking he was jealous, I gave him a flirtatious smile. "What can I say? Men are drawn to me."

Corrigan actually laughed. "Yeah. You *are* a desirable woman, but I wasn't thinking of that guy as competition."

My ego deflated a bit.

Oblivious, he went on. "That attachment could be of use. He may know more than he's letting on. More than he'll tell a cop."

"You think Timothy was involved in his sister's murder?"

"No. But there may be more to the Pittsburgh story, and if you're alone with him, he might tell you."

"You never trust anyone, do you?"

"I'm a cop. I'm paid not to trust people."

"Tough way to live. Anyway, Timothy would tell Gino before he'd tell me. Besides, you didn't want me on this case, remember?" The thought of grilling Timothy in his grieving state under the guise of being his friend didn't sit well with me. "Or is it more expedient to have me involved now?"

Before he would defend his actions, I said, "I've got to get back to the office."

Corrigan frowned. "Claire, I didn't mean you'd have to lie to the guy or anything, and, you're right. I don't want you on this case. But getting more information from Timothy shouldn't be dangerous. It's not like you're going after the killer yourself. If you found out anything important from Timothy, you could let me know. I wouldn't even consider you doing that much, but we need a break on this case before the guy kills again." He gripped my shoulders. "I'd rather take a bullet than have you hurt. I thought you knew that."

I relented on my Corrigan-as-heartless-cop stance.

"Yeah, I do. If Timothy can tell me anything else, I'll let you know." I'm such a pushover for blue eyes, blond hair, and muscles. "Now I really do have to get to the office."

That was the truth and, God help me, I needed to confer with Gino. Maybe he had some ideas.

When I arrived, Betty was gone, and Gino was staring at his computer screen. "Anything new, Gino?" I figured on giving him the Pittsburgh scoop after finding out if he'd learned anything more.

"Nope. Say, did you ever talk to that music teacher? Something Billingham?"

"Donald Billingham. The guy with the cape? Just for a second. Why?"

"Did you know he had some priors? One count of assault. It was dismissed. But he was also convicted of stalking."

"You're kidding!"

He leaned back, fingers interlaced behind his head. "Take a look."

"How could I have missed that?"

"A good PI knows to check and double check information."

I thought about pushing his chair over. "Of course." I pulled my car keys out.

"Where're you going?"

"To double check my information."

Chapter Fourteen

Arriving at Donald Billingham's music store and studio, I tried the door. It was locked and a sign stating a lesson was in session stopped me. Only ninety minutes until bingo started at St. John's Church hall. I didn't have much time to wait. While I was debating whether or not to let Angie know I'd be late, a middle-aged woman exited the store.

"Excuse me, ma'am?"

The well-dressed lady came to a halt. "Yes?"

"Are you taking piano lessons from Mr. Billingham?"

"Yes, I am." She raised her chin. "Why?"

Telling her I was a PI investigating the Red Bow killings wasn't likely to get me the information I wanted. "I'm thinking of taking lessons too. I've heard he's very temperamental."

Her laugh was a practiced tinkle. "Heavens, no. I've been coming to him for three years and he's the sweetest, most patient man I know. We usually sit and gab after my lesson, but this afternoon he cut it short because he's got business that couldn't wait at St. John's Church. He even joked about getting rid of the evidence there."

St. John's? Evidence? Couldn't be a coincidence. I moved ever so slightly towards her and lowered my voice. "You don't happen to play bingo, do you?"

She sniffed. "What does that have to do with anything? If you'll excuse me." She hurried away as if she was afraid whatever possessed me might overtake her too.

I rushed to my car and got in just as Billingham was locking the door to his store. He got into his car, started the engine, and pulled into traffic. Keeping a distance between us, I followed him.

Squirming in my seat, I told myself to take it slow, but the excitement was expanding in me like popcorn in a microwave. Controlling it was going to be difficult. Keeping my eye on Billingham, I speed-dialed Ed, hoping the jitters in my belly would simmer down.

"Hey, kiddo. Whatcha need?"

"Can you meet me at St. John's Church in Lakewood, like now?"

"No-can-do. I'm on my way to work. Switched shifts. Can it wait?"

"No. Guess I'll handle it myself." The agitation in my voice must have alarmed him.

"If this is about the serial killer, don't go in yourself. Call Brian."

My brain was trying to piece together an alternate plan, and I wasn't sure Corrigan figured into it yet. "I'll see what develops first. Talk to you later." Knowing I'd be doing this alone, my stomach sped past jittery. Nausea was next in line. Still, I kept on Billingham's tail.

He pulled into the almost-empty church parking lot and turned off his engine. Not wanting him to see me, I drove past the lot and turned down the alley on the next street. By the time I hoofed it back over, he'd disappeared. The church and its hall where the bingo game was to be held stood side-by-side.

My first guess was that he'd gone into the hall. Pulling out my gun, I charged into the building. The only person there was a man setting up the bingo table. Back out I went and rushed through the front doors of the church. I quickly genuflected and made the Sign of the Cross.

Hearing footsteps above me, I looked around for stairs. There were winding staircases on either side of the pews. I chose the one on the right. My heart was hammering and my mouth was dry as I climbed to the choir loft. Spotting Billingham but not wanting him to see me, I ducked behind a pillar. He was standing by a massive church organ, a red ribbon bunched in his hands. He was quietly speaking with a middle-aged woman in a conservative pantsuit.

No doubt his next victim.

Holding my gun in both hands to steady it, I took a deep breath. I spun away from the pillar and yelled, "Freeze."

The woman yelped and Billingham dropped the

ribbon.

"Okay, put your hands up, Billingham. I'm a private detective working with the Cleveland Police. Ma'am, are you all right?"

The woman put her hands to her chest and was breathing hard. "Goodness, you gave me a start."

Billingham's face turned as red as the ribbon he'd been holding. "What is the meaning of this? I'm here with Mrs. Olecki to inspect the new organ."

Ignoring his protests, I kept the gun on the musician, pulled out my phone and asked the woman to dial 911.

She protested, "I'm fine, really. Just a little startled."

"No need to call anyone." It was Corrigan's voice, yelling from the aisle on the main floor. "I'm coming up."

At the top of the stairs, Corrigan took in the scene; me holding my gun on Billingham, whose arms were up. "What's going on?"

Billingham, Mrs. Olecki, and I all started talking at once. "Hold it!" Corrigan yelled. "Claire, you first."

My words spilled out. "This guy, who just happens to be a piano instructor, had a red ribbon in his hands and he lured this poor woman up here."

Billingham windshielded his arms. "Wait! What? You think I'm that Red Bow fellow? That's absurd. I'm here to inspect this organ. Ask Father Edward. Mrs. Olecki, tell them." He was practically foaming at the mouth. "Please! You have to believe me."

Mrs. Olecki's hands fluttered. "He's telling the truth.

Father Edward asked Mr. Billingham to come and test it out. I let him in. The bow was wrapped around the organ when we arrived. You know, it was a donation from the Knights of Columbus."

Corrigan looked to heaven, probably asking God for patience. "Claire, put the gun down. Mrs. Olecki, please call Father Edward. Put him on speaker phone."

When the priest answered, he verified Mrs. Olecki's story. Billingham was indeed checking the new organ. My face burned as Corrigan apologized to Billingham for the misunderstanding.

Mrs. Olecki chirped. "Imagine if I had been confronted with the Red Bow Killer. Oh, my!"

Billingham was less than gracious. "Detective, I'll let this go. But," he pointed at me. "Keep that mad woman away from me."

I wished the loft had a trapdoor I could drop from. Instead I had to remain under Corrigan's wary watch until Billingham and Mrs. Olecki exited. The musician was still exclaiming how he'd been wronged.

Corrigan glared at me, arms folded across his chest. "How do you do it, Claire?"

"Do what?" I asked in a small voice.

"Manage to mess things up and still keep on going."

"I'm sorry this didn't work out, but what if he had been the killer?"

"Then the police would have found out and arrested him. Without your so-called help."

My tongue wasn't just loose, it was independent of

my brain. Placing my hands on my hips, I sassed, "Yeah, you're doing a great job on your own."

His eyes turned to slits and his jaw clenched. "*Et tu*, Claire?"

I bit my lower lip, knowing I'd gone too far. "I mean, it's a tough case, what with five murders..." Trying to fix it just made it worse.

His voice was deadly calm. "My captain is chewing my ass off to get this killer and I'm running around following up on all these so-called leads, thanks to the media. But I took time out to make sure you were okay." He ran his fingers through his hair. "If I didn't love you..." A deep sigh. "I need to get back to my job, great or not." He turned his back to me and headed toward the stairs.

My face felt as if I had been standing too close to a fire. "Brian, wait! I'm sorry!" I was just about to run after him when he growled and I knew not to follow him.

Anyway, my phone rang. It was Ed.

"Hey, kiddo. Brian get there okay?"

My eyebrows lowered. "You told him to come here?"

"Yep. Now don't get snippy. Figured if that guy was the Red Bow Killer you'd need some help."

Squeezing my phone so hard my knuckles turned white, I said, "I understand, but it didn't work out so well. The man I followed here isn't the killer." Not wanting to go into detail I ended the call by saying, "Bingo game is starting. I don't want to miss it."

Which was true, but it was the coward's way of exiting my own comedy of errors.

Angie was waiting for me in the church hall vestibule, holding two bingo cards and markers. "They've already started the first game, but we can still go in."

I was so distressed with my faux pas and Corrigan's reaction I didn't even pay attention to where Angie sat us. By the time the first winner read her numbers aloud, I stopped feeling as if I should prostrate myself in front of Corrigan and beg his forgiveness. I was here to do a job. Making up with Corrigan would have to wait. That is, if he was willing to make up.

Angie and I sat next to each other watching others in the room while also attending to our bingo cards. This evening there were two men who could physically be the Red Bow Killer, meaning they were under the age of eighty and had no debilitating issues. While everyone else was occupied with their cards and the numbers called, I snapped pictures of the two.

Angie leaned toward me and whispered, "What do we do now?" The woman next to her shushed her and the elderly man across from Angie threw a disapproving glance her way.

I held up my index finger to indicate waiting until this game was over.

The host picked a bingo tile and announced, "G-53. G as in Gary 53."

A fortyish woman let out a whoop and screamed she

had bingo. While she and the host went over the numbers, I reviewed what we were looking for, not only a man physically capable of strangling a woman but who seemed unusually interested in any one of the players here. "In case we need them, we have pictures. Between games we can ask the deacon their names. We don't talk to them directly. Okay?"

Angie jutted her chin. "That's it?"

The next game was starting and I didn't have a chance to elaborate. Of course, that was if there was anything to elaborate on. Speaking out loud about what I was doing actually sounded lame. Maybe I needed to rethink this.

But not now. A white-haired man entered the room and slowly shuffled to an empty chair at a back table. I pressed my lips together hard, trying to remember where I'd seen him before. PI's should have great recall for faces. Ignoring my bingo card, I tapped my forehead, as if that would loosen the memory. It didn't.

While I was involved in this exercise, Angie won the game and the frown she'd been wearing morphed into a grin. "This is the first game I've won. It must be because of you."

I chuckled, "Glad to be your good-luck charm." But fear that Angie's winning made her more of a target wiped away any trace of humor.

Realizing it was time for me to head to *Cannoli's,* I took one last look around the room. My eyes settled on the elderly man I'd noticed earlier and my head jerked back slightly as it hit me. His name was Jerry. He was the guy who had been friendly with Eileen at Smalley's. Was the world that small or did his presence here have anything to do with the murders? Not that he looked like a killer. Too fragile and he moved so slowly the victim could run home and change clothes before he reached her.

My aunt was surely waiting for me, but I couldn't leave. Not yet. The next game had already started so without taking the time to provide her with details, I tilted my head toward Jerry's table. "The old guy there?" Angie nodded. "Keep an eye on him. See if he's with someone, or someone picks him up. Get his license plate number if you can. Don't approach him, though."

"He's your suspect?" Angie's eyes widened.

Our tablemates were beyond throwing us dirty looks and the guy across from me actually told me to shut up.

Again, there was no time to explain my reasoning to Angie, so I merely nodded. I pushed back my chair to take my leave just as one of the women at our table yelled bingo. I sneaked out while her numbers were being reviewed. My plan was to first attend to Charlie and then make it on time to my second job.

All the way to *Cannoli's,* I second-guessed myself. Should I have stayed and watched Jerry myself? From there, my conscience imagined Angie beaten and bloody, victim of Jerry's hidden viciousness and cunning. I brooded over it all and as soon as I pulled into *Cannoli's* parking lot, I called Angie, praying she'd be able to answer her phone.

"Claire? Did you forget something?" To my relief, Angie sounded unhurt.

"No, I just…"

"I'm fine and I even had a quick conversation with Jerry. The guy you told me to watch. His neighbor picked him up after only one game, so I had to act fast. Anyway, he said his nephew whom he lives with, usually does, but he was busy tonight."

Relieved she was okay, I nonetheless was frustrated, wondering what part of 'don't approach him' she didn't understand. Resigning myself to her actions, I asked, "Did you get any other information, like his last name? Or his nephew's name?"

"Jerry said his last name, but he talked so low, I had to ask him twice. It's Malden. And I'll talk to both of those other guys before the evening's over."

"Well, that's a start. Thanks, Angie." As an afterthought, I added, "Don't forget. Don't leave the bingo hall until your son pulls in—"

"I know, in front of the building. I'll be fine, Claire. Better go, the next game is starting."

With the call ended, I walked into *Cannoli's,* just in time to witness a disgruntled Aunt Lena, arms crossed, gripping a large wooden rolling pin.

Chapter Fifteen

Usually I greet my aunt with a quick kiss on the cheek. Judging by the look on her face, this time I decided to keep my distance. Drawing the conclusion she discovered my lying about skipping work at *Cannoli's*, I didn't want her to see my oh-so-guilty expression. "Hi, Aunt Lena."

When her response was a harrumph, I slipped an apron over my head as if it could protect me from her wrath. I searched for a way to explain the lies without getting punished for them.

She harrumphed again and waved the rolling pin at me. "I know what you've been doing and it stops right now. You hear me?"

I could have dropped to my knees and confessed all. Instead I took the coward's way and inquired angelically, "What are you talking about?" I tried, but failed to make eye contact.

She lowered the pin to her side. "You know very well. You've been telling people I'm a nervous wreck and you've had to pick up the slack, frosting cupcakes for me even." Her chin trembled.

Relieved this wasn't about me lying and missing work, I was obviously still to blame. "What?" Then I recalled using that as an excuse to Gino. *Who had he told?* "Aunt Lena, I'm so sorry! I needed an excuse as to why I wasn't in the office. I never imagined Gino would say anything…" My voice trailed off.

She sniffed, a sure sign I wasn't forgiven. "Well, that blabbermouth told somebody, who told somebody else. Anyway, this morning Gloria Valducci, that barracuda you did catering work for, offered to buy me out. Said she understood the business could be too hard for a woman my age. *My* age? Gloria's six months older than me!"

Casting my eyes downward in penitence I asked, "How can I make it up to you?"

"Stop telling that idiot boss of yours anything about me. Even true stuff." She shook her head. "What kind of private detective can't keep his mouth shut? Maybe you should quit and work full time here. I could use your help."

I stifled a groan. *Same conversation, different day.* I put my arm around her shoulder. "You know I love you and working here is great, but—"

She interrupted, "I know, I know." She lay down her rolling pin. "Well, let's get busy. Customers are already waiting."

Time flew as I plated and boxed cupcakes, éclairs, and cake slices for the many people demanding to satisfy their sweet tooth. In fact, I barely noticed the hour until Angie called me at eight.

"Claire, I did what you asked me to do." She sounded excited, almost breathless. "I got the names of those two men. In fact, I had a conversation with each of them."

I closed my eyes to calm myself. She'd obviously forgotten she wasn't supposed to talk to either of the men. The last thing I wanted was for Angie to be on the possible killer's radar. "You didn't give either of them any personal information, did you?"

Silence on Angie's end told me I wasn't going to like her answer. "Well, the second one asked me out."

My chest tightened. "You turned him down, didn't you?"

"Nope. Now don't worry. We're meeting tomorrow evening for dinner at Palacio's."

Through clenched teeth I said, "He could wrap you up with a ribbon by the time you get from your car to the restaurant. I'm coming with you."

"That's not necessary. He seems like a decent guy."

"I'm sure that's what they said about Vlad the Impaler. Maybe Brian can come, so it'll be like a double date."

"Oka-a-y. I'll let Norm know."

"No. We'll just be there when he shows up. What time are you meeting?"

"At seven."

"Got it. Now what about that other guy?"

"Nice man. He teaches at St. Mary's. Fifth grade. Get

this. He used to be a friar."

I wrinkled my nose. "Doesn't exactly fit my impression of a serial killer. Either of these men play instruments?"

"Friar Tuck doesn't. Norm plays the accordion in a wedding band."

"What's Norm's last name? I'll check him out."

"Norm Rockwell."

"You're kidding, right?"

"No. He even showed me his driver's license."

I blew a breath into my bangs. "Okay. Are you home?"

"Yeah. Safe and sound."

Relief cascaded through me. "Good. Lock your doors and don't let anyone in. Not even Norm. Also, thank you. I'll see you tomorrow evening."

She tsk'd, "You're worse than my mother. Next you'll be after me about wearing my dresses too short."

I laughed. "Been meaning to tell you…" My aunt threw me a look as some customers were walking in, so with a quick goodbye, I hung up.

As Aunt Lena rang up an order of six cupcakes, she wanted to know who I was talking to. "It sounded like Angie, but why would she call you?"

"She has a date tomorrow night with this guy she met and thought I might know him." I cringed inside, afraid she'd call my bluff.

Instead, Aunt Lena's cherub-round face lit up like a kid getting into the Halloween candy. "What's he like?"

"Don't know much about him except his name is Norm and he plays the accordion."

My aunt's look of excitement turned into frustration. "Too bad I gotta be here. I'd like to meet this guy. You know, show up at the restaurant and give him the once-over. For Angie's sake. Last time she had a date, Clinton was president."

I cut my laugh short when I realized she was serious. "I'll get you the low down on him."

Two portly women came up to the counter, interrupting our conversation. "Excuse me, but we're in a hurry. We need to get home before it's too late."

It was past eight thirty and *Cannoli's* closed at nine.

The other lady concurred. "As good as the éclairs are here, I'd hate for them to be my last meal."

Normally I don't pay a lot of attention to what customers say. Just smile and nod. This conversation had me wondering. I didn't need to wonder long. Though the four of us were the only ones in *Cannoli's* the larger of the two women lowered her voice. "That Red Bow Killer got another one tonight. Somewhere around 117th and Detroit."

My throat tightened and I felt a bit dizzy. I prayed Angie had been telling the truth about being home. Trying to keep my voice steady, I asked, "Have you heard anything else?"

The other woman's eyes bulged. "Isn't that enough? How can any woman feel safe? What are the cops doing? Eating donuts, I bet."

My temper rose but I clamped it down. “I happen to know the cops are doing all they can to find this monster.”

My aunt was wringing her hands. “That’s it. We’re closing, ladies. Here’re your éclairs.” She slid the box across the counter. “Be careful going home.”

She followed them to the door and locked it. “I’m calling Ed to pick me up. We’ll follow you home. You’re not going to walk into that apartment alone.”

A bit uneasy myself, I agreed to her plan. Then I called Angie, just to double-check she was home and safe.

“Claire, I told you I was home. Why would I lie?”

“There’s been another murder. I just had to make sure it wasn’t you.”

She let out a shaky breath. “It wasn’t.” She paused. “Thanks for being concerned, though.”

Worries over Angie alleviated, my mind jumped to wondering about the victim. Was she a bingo player? Could she have been somebody from St. John’s? The crime scene wasn’t that far from the church. My legs wobbled like bowling pins just before they topple over. Another thought flashed through my head. How was Corrigan dealing with yet one more murder?

While Aunt Lena called Ed and requested his protective presence, I cleaned up. Once she was off the phone she joined me, but neither of us talked. That was just as well since undoubtedly our conversation would have returned to the Red Bow Killer’s latest victim.

Once Ed arrived, he and my aunt walked me to my car and followed me home. Ed even escorted me to my door. "Lock up, kiddo. Your aunt's paranoid about this killer getting someone she loves. Don't make her right to have worried."

Obediently, I dead-bolted my door behind him and opened the cage for Charlie. Poor guy had been confined all day, except for the quick pit stop I'd made before going to *Cannoli's*.

After he covered me with puppy licks, he stood by the door. I sighed and picked up his leash. Pulling my gun from my purse, I told myself the killer already did his deed for tonight. Still, I hoped Charlie would do his stuff in record time.

The dog must have had momentary mind-reading capabilities because he got right down to business. Then he looked at me like he wanted nothing more than to be back inside. Maybe he sensed my unease. No matter the cause, as soon as I closed the door behind us, we both seemed to relax.

Grabbing a cup of tea and some treats for Charlie, we reclined on the sofa and turned the television on. I should have just gone to bed.

A freshly-shaven news reporter was at the scene of the latest murder, talking with a woman who was wearing something that looked like pajamas. He asked her to describe what happened that evening.

"Well, my husband, Fred, and me was sitting on the porch, smoking. Meanwhile that poor lady musta come upon the corpse and let out a scream. Blood curdling, it was. We rushed toward the sound. First, we seen the woman who found the body and then the actual body with a ribbon tied around the neck. It was horrible. Fred called 911 and I comforted the woman who happened on it."

The reporter nodded, hanging on every word the interviewee said. He thanked her and was ready to return the broadcast to the station when that same witness grabbed the microphone. "Where was the cops? They're supposed to protect us. None of us women is safe 'til this maniac gets caught or killed."

The reporter wrestled the microphone away from the woman. Then, "Back to you, Melissa."

The anchor, Melissa Perfect-Hair-And-Makeup, sitting behind a desk on the studio set, shook her head. "Thank you, Brad." She paused and put on her serious face. "Cleveland women are becoming more frightened, while the police seem to have no suspects in this string of killings. This is the sixth victim of the Red Bow Killer. Her name has been withheld pending family notification."

My heart beat in sympathy and sorrow for the victim and her family. Nobody deserved that ending. My sympathy extended to Corrigan as well. Recalling my less-than-supportive last comment to him, my face burned hot enough to cook pasta. Now, with this latest murder, he'd be so busy there'd be no way of knowing when I'd be able apologize. I moaned and Charlie, taking it as a signal, began to lick my face and for an instant made me forget my guilt.

When it was finally time for bed, Charlie refused to go back into his cage. Not that I blamed him. Poor thing spent so much time in there. Plus, I could use a living creature next to me, even if it was covered in fur and had Kibbles breath.

Charlie slept soundly, which is more than I could say for myself. Frustrated with doing nothing but tossing back and forth, I finally arose at four and shuffled off to the living room to do some work.

Wiping any remnants of sleep from my eyes, I flicked on my computer and flipped through the latest news to see if there was anything else on the most recent victim. While I was wading through all the online gossip, Charlie trotted over, pawed me, and went to the door. It was a good time for a break. Between all the wild speculations and the complaints about the cops, my patience was wearing as thin as a Supermodel's arms. I grabbed the leash and we headed outside.

My phone rang just as Charlie decided he needed a sprint. Off we went after something only he saw. I finally got him to stop and answered my phone. It was Corrigan.

"You're up?" As so often lately, he sounded exhausted.

"Yes. Charlie had to answer nature's call." I pulled on the leash and we turned toward home. "What's up?" I winced over my inane question. What did I *think* was up?

"You no doubt heard. Another victim. Do you have

some time to spare?"

Now that Charlie figured out what we were doing, he didn't want to wait and so began dragging me to the apartment. My voice bounced as we ran. "Sure. Is this about the latest victim?"

"I'll explain when I see you. Be there in about twenty minutes."

Twenty minutes? It'd take me that long to rub the sleep creases from my face. "Yeah, that's good."

We hung up and Charlie and I raced to the apartment. He was probably hungry but my desire to look presentable pushed me. Still, he was happily chomping down on his puppy food when Corrigan knocked.

I opened the door and tried to hide my surprise. He looked like he'd been living in the trunk of his car. His suit hung limply, as if it was as tired as its wearer. Usually clean-shaven, his blond whiskers made his face look fuzzy, blurring the lines of his chin and cheeks. The dullness in his eyes was what tore at my heart the most. The poor guy needed a break in the case and more time after that to recuperate.

"Come in, Brian." I led him in by the arm and he offered no resistance. I'd never seen him so cowed and it almost frightened me. Then, shame and regret over my last insult to him overcame me and I blurted out, "What I said to you about the job you're doing. I didn't mean it, really."

He dismissed my apology with a weak wave of his hand. "Forget it. It's nowhere near the worst I've heard lately."

"Okay." Shifting from one leg to the other, "Let's sit down. Want some tea or something to eat?"

"Thanks, no." At least he took up my offer to sit. He pulled out his notepad. "I need you to tell me about the bingo game at St. John's yesterday evening. I assume you were there."

I squinted, my mind spinning like the cage holding the bingo tiles. "You think the latest victim was playing bingo there last night?"

He sank back into the sofa. "She played bingo somewhere and St. John's is a good place to start. It's close to where her body was found. Plus, she had some daubers in her purse. They're like markers—"

"I know what they are. So you think she was at St. John's."

"You tell me." He pulled out a picture of the victim. Like the others, she had a ribbon tied into a bow around her neck.

Biting down on my lower lip, I recalled the slender woman who sat across from me at bingo. She had won the last game before I left. Tightly intertwining my fingers, I nodded.

He placed one of his hands over mine. "Did you notice anybody who looked or acted strange in any way? Did someone act aggressively toward the victim, or show a lot of interest in her?"

"Not that I noticed. There were only two men in the place that looked even capable of strangling someone.

Just a minute." My legs felt as if they'd give out when I stood, but not wanting Corrigan to see my faintheartedness, I continued toward my phone.

Once it was in my hands, I plopped back down on the sofa, took a breath, and showed him the first of the two photos I'd taken last evening.

"This first guy was a friar." I repeated the rest of what Angie had told me about him and then switched photos to Norm's. "Besides bingo, this one also plays an instrument. Accordion. His name is Norm Rockwell."

Corrigan's upper lip went into an Elvis curl. "Gotta be an alias."

"It matches his driver's license. Furthermore, he has a date with Angie Frankowsky, Aunt Lena's friend. She was at bingo last night with me. In fact, she stayed until the end, so she might have even seen if the victim left with anyone."

His face revealed nothing. He merely asked, in a level professional tone, "Do you have Angie's address? I'll need to question her too."

"Sure. Anyway, Angie and this Norm are meeting at Palacio's on Center Ridge at 7:00 tonight." At the last minute I decided not to ask him to come along. Maybe it was because he looked so tired and worn. He didn't need a working dinner. "She'll have company. Me." That had sounded a lot cleverer in my head.

The vein in his temple boogied, and I doubted he'd give up any information about the latest victim. "You've got to be kidding! You and Angie can't be thinking of meeting up with this guy." He must have decided I wasn't kidding because he paused and smoothed down his hair. "Hey, changed my mind. Can I have some tea?"

"Of course." Sensing an advantage, I wasn't about to pour him anything without first driving home my point. "We'll be fine. It's a public place and I'll have my gun." He didn't argue so I grew bolder. "Okay, what else do you know about last night's victim?"

"Tea first."

He followed me into the kitchen. While I was boiling the water, he began to heat up my hormones by wrapping his arms around me and nuzzling my neck. From the feel of things, he'd found a way to rejuvenate himself, or he was stalling. Although the first option was more flattering to me, the real reason didn't matter. I wanted some answers. "This is nice, but you haven't told me anything."

He just murmured into my neck.

My voice firm, "Brian."

He backed off. "Victim's name was Shirley Dolecek, sixty years old, widowed. Only child killed in Afghanistan. The deceased's sister lives in Chicago, but she'll be in town later today. We're still in the process of piecing the events together."

Keeping my hands steady enough to pour the tea was impossible. Six women killed in such a short time and this last one had been at the same bingo hall, even the same table as Angie and me. I hadn't known the woman, but her being so near to me shortly before her death made it feel almost personal, as if I were being attacked.

Corrigan poured the tea. He blew on his cup and as soon as it cooled he took a sip. Putting it down, he sighed, "Better get going. My partner and I are both meeting with the Captain later this morning. No doubt he's planning on motivating us by screaming at the top of his lungs."

He kissed me hard and asked, "Would you love me if I was back in uniform?" His joke was tinged with worry.

My heart crumbled like a too-crisp chocolate chip cookie. Throwing my arms around his neck, "I'd love you if you wore a janitor's uniform."

He nodded and walked out. Closing the door behind him, I slid to the floor. Charlie, no doubt spotting a play opportunity, pushed open the unlocked door of his cage and, trotted over, licking and nipping at me. I grabbed him and chuckled in spite of myself. "Come on, Charlie. I'm already late for work. Let's have breakfast. Chocolate for me and puppy food for you."

My phone rang, spoiling my meal plan. It was Angie. I barely had time to say hello before she began.

"Did you see that latest victim? She sat at the same bingo table as us." Her voice shook, but she continued with a bravado I admired, "That means we're close to finding the creep."

"Yes, but we still don't know who the killer is. By the way, this last victim's name was Shirley Dolecek. Did you see her leave? Was she alone?"

"To tell you the truth, she left without me noticing. I

keep thinking, I could've walked with her to her car or something. I'm kicking myself for that." Her voice grew solemn. "She'd still be living if I had paid more attention to her."

I couldn't let Angie beat herself up. "Don't think like that. If you had gotten in the middle of it, you could have ended up as victim number seven."

Still, I understood how she felt. There have been times that same regret stuck in my head and nobody could talk me out of it. No sense in belaboring it, though. "One more thing. Corrigan was just here. Expect a visit. Please don't tell him you're working with me, though. He's already worried about my involvement. He doesn't need to worry about yours, too."

"Mum's the word. Anyway, I don't want it getting back to Lena." She paused and her voice took on her familiar stubborn quality. "I'm still going out with Norm."

"Okay, but don't forget I'm going too."

She groaned, "He's not the killer. I don't get that kind of vibe from him."

"I'm picking you up at six thirty. I bet the victims didn't get a vibe about the killer either. Something you learn in this business; suspect everyone."

She snorted, "Yeah, okay. I can see how that way of thinking comes in handy. Well, time to go to work. If you told Lena about Norm she'll have a million questions."

Breakfast, even though it was chocolate, didn't

appeal to me anymore, but I promised Charlie his, so I fed him and then headed to the office. It was already nine but experience told me Gino wouldn't be in.

He wasn't. Just as well, I wasn't in the mood to have him offer the sage advice he believed he always gave. Adding Shirley Dolecek to my list of victims didn't exactly put me into a happy frame of mind. The now-familiar questions haunted me. What was it about bingo that set the killer off? Was music a trigger that the killer controlled most of the time, but sometimes let it set him off? *Why? Why? Why?*

I leaned forward in my chair and stared at the computer screen as if the closer I got to it the clearer the answers. The only answer I got was no answer. I had to do something. My music lesson wasn't until next week, but all of a sudden I wasn't willing to wait that long to press Todd Shotswell. He still had my vote for person-of-interest.

Leaving a note for Gino that said I'd waited all morning for him, off I went.

Lucky for me, there was only one customer in Shotswell's store and the guy was just leaving.

Todd gave me one of his charming smiles. "Claire! How nice to see you again. Is there something you need?" His smile morphed into a look of concern. "I hope you haven't changed your mind about your lessons."

It'd be easy to let my guard down with this guy. That is, if he wasn't on my radar as a likely candidate for serial killer. "Oh, no. Not at all. I just wanted to ask you if, um, if it'd make a difference if I started my lessons with a tenor sax instead. See, my dad has one and I could pick it up on my way to bingo. I play bingo all the time."

I'm not quite sure what I expected, but it wasn't another one of those smiles. "If you'd rather start with a tenor, that's fine. It might be a little harder at first, though. Bring in the rental sax and I'll give you a refund."

He wasn't taking the bait, so I loaded another worm on the hook. "Do you play bingo? It's a lot of fun. Once I learn the saxophone, I'll be playing my two favorite things."

Although that sounded lame even to me, he was polite. "No, I'm sorry. I don't play. Some of my relatives did, or do."

"Oh, yes. Lots of people do. Mostly women, but some men. Any men in your family? I mean, any men who play bingo?" Now he was looking at me as if I were slightly unhinged.

"My mother used to play. And her brother, my uncle."

The bell on his door sounded. "Will you excuse me? I have another customer, but I'll see you next week." He closed the music book, as if dismissing me.

Taking the hint, I slunk out of the store and walked stiffly to my car. Once inside I leaned my head against my steering wheel. "Stupid, stupid." I stopped. His uncle played bingo. Maybe he was musical too. I headed back to work determined to look into his uncle's life. *Could both he and his uncle be involved in a serial killer duet?*

***

Gino was sitting at his desk, tapping a pen against his keyboard. "Hey Claire, come and take a look at this."

Wondering if he'd even noticed I'd been gone I dropped my purse and went into his office. On his computer screen was a video of Shirley Dolecek at a party of some sort. She was playing the piano. He paused the video. "Now all we have to do is find out if she played bingo."

"Got that covered, boss. She was last seen at a bingo game."

He swiveled his chair to face me. "Get out! That solves it, then. We need to stake out some local bingo parlors. See who's hanging out at them."

I took a long breath in and out, calming myself. "A friend of mine and I've been doing that. Nothing so far."

"Maybe you just haven't been observant enough."

It was all I could do not to grab my bingo card marker and dot his face with it. "We have. In fact, tonight, my friend and I are meeting somebody who might be a suspect."

One of his eyebrows rose. "Is that safe? You think he's our guy?"

"It's at Palacio's at seven. Prime dinner time. We'll be fine."

Almost to himself, "Could be the break we need to solve this case."

We? “Well, I won’t know anything until I question him.” The last thing I wanted was Gino to bypass facts to get to the reward.

The rest of the day went slowly as I filed and made business calls for Gino. In between my work duties, I tried to uncover more about Shotswell’s uncle, but since he had a different last name, unknown first, and I had no address, I had no luck. Nor was I able to come up with any motive for killing six women. By the end of the day, all the filing was done and the calls made, but I was still no closer to having a motive or information on the uncle.

I consoled myself with imagining it would all fall into place tonight with Norm confessing he was the killer.

Before leaving the office, I called my aunt to remind her I wouldn’t be at *Cannoli’s* tonight.

“That’s okay. Your father’s coming to help out.”

“That’s great, Aunt Lena. See you tomorrow night.” Then I was on my way home to first check on Charlie, then freshen up and head out to Palacio’s. Just in case, I also double-checked that my gun was loaded.

Chapter Sixteen

Angie walked ahead of me into Palacio's. She was wearing a green sheath dress that showed off her green eyes and her still-good figure. Part of me hoped this guy wasn't the murderer. It'd be nice for Angie to have someone. On the other hand, if he was the Red Bow Killer, we'd get him behind bars and the women in Cleveland and its suburbs could relax. Plus, I'd get at least half of the reward Smalley's was offering

While we waited just inside the restaurant door, I said, "You look very nice, Angie."

She smiled and brushed a strand of her heavily-sprayed hair from her forehead. "Thanks. To tell you the truth, my nerves are doing a jitterbug." Before I could say anything, she added, "Not because I think he's the killer. He can't be. It's because I haven't had a date in a long time." She paused, "You know, today when Corrigan was questioning me about the bingo game, it hit me again how truly gorgeous your guy is. And polite. Hang on to that one, Claire. He's a keeper."

It was my turn to smile. "Yeah. I plan to. If he's

agreeable, could be for the rest of my life."

The maitre d appeared and offered to escort us to our table, but wanting to take note of the kind of car Norm drove, I put the host off.

About five minutes later, "That's him. That's Norm." Angie's fluttering hands unnecessarily smoothed her dress.

A familiar-looking man stepped out of a dark sedan and handed the keys to the valet. He was taller and bulkier than I recalled, and well-dressed.

As soon as he came through the door, Angie made the introductions. "Claire's boyfriend couldn't make it so I told her it'd be fine if we were a trio instead of a duo."

A look of surprise and perhaps disappointment skipped across his face, but he quickly recovered. "I consider myself a lucky man tonight being in the company of two beautiful women."

Chalk one up for Norm. He knew how to handle a situation that didn't go according to plan. Or did that just prove he was a successful serial killer? With some skill, luck and feminine wiles I might find out before another woman died. I was glad I didn't get around to asking Corrigan to join us. Maybe Norm would be more relaxed and open with just two women asking questions.

We were seated and as soon as we placed our drink orders, I began. "So, Norm, how long have you been playing bingo?"

"I go once in a while. It gets me out of the house. I'm not a nightlife kind of guy so bars don't interest me.

Neither do the people that frequent them." He placed his napkin on his lap. "I'm in a band but we usually just play weddings and anniversary parties. Not much call for an accordion in a rock band." He laughed, revealing crooked but white teeth.

I couldn't stop myself. "So do you think the women who play bingo are nice?"

"Sometimes. Like Angie here."

"Did you know Joanna Whitechapel? She sometimes went by the name of Desiree."

"I bet she's talking your ear off, isn't she?" I looked up and saw the clean-shaven face of my favorite detective. Except he wasn't my favorite at that moment.

Corrigan grabbed the back of the empty chair at our table for four.

I hissed, "What are you doing here?"

He ignored me and addressed Norm. "I'm Brian, Claire's boyfriend, although you wouldn't know by her greeting. You must be Norm." He stuck out his hand. "Nice to meet you."

Norm smiled vaguely and shook Corrigan's hand. "How do you do?" The man was definitely polite.

Corrigan grinned like a life insurance salesman in the aisle seat of a full plane. He knew his audience was captive. "So Claire tells me you play bingo and the accordion."

Angie interjected, "I'm famished. Why don't we order some appetizers?"

Ignoring her suggestion, Corrigan went on drilling

like a sadistic dentist. "What do you think of women who stay out either at a bar listening to music or play bingo instead of taking care of their families?"

"I…I hadn't thought about it." He took a sip of his drink.

"It doesn't make you mad?"

Norm's face turned a bit splotchy. "I suppose people should do what's best for their loved ones."

Corrigan continued with, "What did you do after you talked to Angie last night at bingo?"

Norm shrugged. "What I always do. I went home and read for a while."

"You live alone?" Corrigan was going in for the kill.

"Yes. Are you asking me because of that woman who was murdered?"

I shoved a menu in front of Corrigan before he could answer and followed that by glaring at him. "I think ordering appetizers is a great idea. Why don't we each pick one and we can share."

A voice behind me said, "That's the best idea I've heard all day." I closed my eyes and slowly turned around in my chair before opening them. Standing there were my aunt and Ed. Ed gave me a look that made it clear this hadn't been his idea.

When the waiter was done setting down the drinks for Angie, Norm, and me, Aunt Lena asked him, "Could we get a bigger table so all of us can sit together?" She looked at Norm and said, "This way we can get to know you."

Angie covered her eyes with her hand. Norm glanced around as if to make sure this was really happening.

Drinks, menus, and napkins in hand, we switched tables. Aunt Lena insisted on Norm sitting between her and Angie.

Ed murmured to me, “I tried to talk her out of busting into this dinner.”

Thankfully the waiter came back and asked the newcomers for their drink orders. Otherwise, who knows what words would have escaped from my mouth?

Ed ordered a beer. Aunt Lena smiled pleasantly. “I’ll have a Pink Lady.” After the waiter left, my aunt waved her hand. “Go ahead with what you were talking about before we got here. Oh, but by the way, Norm, I hear you play the accordion.”

Norm sighed, as if relieved for moving off the topic of the murdered woman. “Yes, I play both the button and the piano type accordions.”

Angie finally spoke, “I didn’t realize there were two types.”

Norm started to warm up. “Oh, yes. And there’s even more differentiation than that.”

At almost the same time, Corrigan and I asked, “Do you play other instruments?”

He shook his head, “No. Used to play piano, but it’s easier to carry an accordion with me.”

Lena didn’t allow him to pause for a breath. “Have you ever been married, Norm?”

“Aunt Lena, what’s that got to do with the

accordion?"

She huffed, "Well, he plays at weddings. Women are already in the mood for romance. And they go crazy for musicians. I remember my crush on Frankie Valli."

Norm's face turned as red as marinara sauce. "No. I've never been married. Haven't met the right woman."

Aunt Lena harrumphed. "Or maybe you're too picky. Take Angie here—"

"That's enough!" Angie threw her napkin down. "Norm, you and I are going over to another table and have our drinks and dinner like we planned. The rest of you can stay here and imagine what we're talking about." She motioned to the waiter, who hustled over.

Norm's eyes lit up. "I like a woman with spunk."

"Then you'll love Angie." My aunt murmured.

Before the newly-formed couple could make a move, another voice boomed, "Hey, where's everybody going? We just got here." It was Gino, accompanied by Betty.

I slunk in my chair while Angie glared at me.

Oblivious to the dynamics of the group, Gino offered his hand to Norm. "You must be the guy Angie picked up at the bingo parlor last night. Name's Gino." Norm, to his credit, shook hands with Gino and said hello. Gino motioned to everyone at the table. "This here is Betty. Betty, you know Claire. Detective Corrigan is next to her, then Lena and her husband, Ed. The older woman next to Norm is Angie."

Betty, in a slinky magenta sequined number better suited to Las Vegas than to Palacio's, gave a general,

"Hi, Everyone. Nice to meetcha."

Our waiter, patiently standing there, in a flustered voice asked if we would all like to move to a bigger table.

"Not on your life." Angie shot back at the poor man. "The newcomers can have our seats." She pointed to Norm. "We'd like another table. For two."

"Make that four." Aunt Lena added, daring Angie to disagree with her.

I was ready to bury my head in my hands, but rising to the occasion, I took a chance. "Ladies, we're all going to powder our noses."

Betty was the only one to object. "But I just got here."

Aunt Lena took Betty by the arm. "Honey, you could use some powder to tone that dress down."

Angie stomped ahead of us and waited until we all piled into the tiny ladies' room. "I don't agree with it, but I know why Claire is here. Why are the rest of you?"

Betty turned red, her complexion clashing with her gown. "I told Gino I didn't want to come. But he said it was my opportunity to come face-to-face with my sister's killer."

Lena spun halfway around and pushed her face so close to Angie's they almost touched noses. "This guy's a killer? Angie, there're dating sites for older—"

Angie threw up her hands. "He's not a killer. He happens to like bingo and plays an accordion. That's it."

I could only hope it was going better at the dinner

table. “Stop it! Everyone, Angie is on a date with Norm—”

My aunt jumped in, “—who just happens to fit the profile of a serial killer.”

“That’s not what I was going to say. He’s not a suspect, or even a person of interest.” I added to myself that he could be, depending on his answers to Corrigan’s questions.

“Thank you, Claire.” Angie looked worn out. “He’s a nice man who happened to think I was a nice woman. That opinion is probably long gone now.”

My aunt sighed and put her beefy arm around Angie’s shoulder. “Angie, we’ve been friends since grade school. Me and Ed came to meet the guy you think is special enough to go out with. If he’s really a good guy then great. I’ll treat him like a brother. If he’s a *sfacimma,* a bad guy, he belongs in prison, not with you.”

Wrapping her arms around herself, Betty asked, “So did he kill my sister Rose, or not?”

I broke the news to her as gently as possible. “Betty, we don’t know anything yet. I’m sorry Gino jumped the gun.” All along I’d felt sorry for her because her sister was dead. Now I felt even sorrier for her because she actually believed Gino would find Rose’s killer.

To my surprise, tears formed in her eyes. “I just want justice for my sister.” Her chin trembled, reminding me this wasn’t just about collecting a reward or avenging Mrs. Amato’s death.

All I could manage was, “We’ll catch the guy. I

know we will."

Angie blew out a deep breath. "Okay, ladies, we're going back out, asking for a bigger table, and acting like this is a friendly gathering. Claire and I will do the serious questioning later."

I muttered, "If we haven't already scared him silent."

The waiter had thoughtfully transferred our party to the back of the room. When we arrived at the table, Norm and Ed were in a debate about which accordion was the best. "Norm, I respect your opinion, but I gotta say, a chromatic button accordion has always sounded great to me."

Norm stood when Angie sat down. Following suit, Ed and Corrigan rose. Gino remained seated until Betty whacked his shoulder. He popped up and remained standing longer than the other men. I revised my opinion of Betty. She was no lamb.

Dessert was being served when Gino, having had three gin and tonics, asked Norm, "So, why do you think that Bow Killer is killing all those poor women?"

Angie glared at Gino. "Why do *you* think he's doing it, Gino?"

Norm's eyes narrowed. "No, I'll give it a shot. Maybe he thought the women disrespected him and he didn't know how else to get his point across." He finished his drink. "Is that what you wanted to hear?" His face got blotchy and he waved to the waiter. "Check please." He faced Angie. "You're a lovely woman, but—
"

Ed jumped in. "Hey, Norm. You shoulda seen what I went through with this group. Nothing personal. They're great when you get to know them."

Norm shook his head as he paid cash for his dinner and Angie's.

I flashed a grateful look at Ed and opened my mouth to take over, but Gino was faster.

"Hey no offense meant, but you were at the right place, right time, right, buddy?"

Angie clenched her fists, no doubt wishing she could plant one on Gino's chin. "I understand, Norm. I'll walk you to your car."

"I'll go too." I couldn't help myself. What if getting Angie alone and defenseless was his plan all along?

Angie responded with a terse, "No. Come on, Norm."

Out of the corner of his mouth, he said, "If you're sure I'm not going to strangle you in the parking lot."

"I am."

The two left the table and headed to the exit.

Corrigan hesitated one moment and threw down some money. "This should cover it for Claire and me." He headed after Angie and Norm only to be waylaid by a beyond tipsy woman from another table who grabbed his arm. Seconds passed and I don't know what she said, but he responded by flashing his badge. She released his arm.

"I'll settle up, Ed." Aunt Lena said as Ed pushed back his chair. Even Gino wove his way toward the exit, leaving my aunt, Betty and me staring at each other. But I couldn't sit there with the womenfolk. I grabbed my purse, which held my gun and out I went, ignoring Aunt Lena's pleas to return to the table.

I caught up with Corrigan, Ed, and Gino, who had each ignored the valet's offers. Instead we dashed across the street to the restaurant's parking lot. Even though we were no more than five minutes behind them, we didn't spot Angie or Norm.

My dinner curdled in my stomach. "He took her. We've got to find them before it's too late!"

Corrigan went into cop mode. "Do you know the make or model of his car?"

"Dark, either blue or black, a Ford sedan." I swallowed hard, my drink threatening to reappear. "This is my fault. I shouldn't have gotten Angie involved."

"We'll get her back."

Corrigan was already on his phone when Ed yelled, "There's Angie now."

"Thank God!" I hustled back across the street, dodging a speeding valet who was driving a Porsche into the lot. Since the men chose caution over quickness, I reached Angie first.

"Angie, where'd you go? Are you all right?" She nodded and without a word handed me a folded-up photograph. She seemed in a daze.

Opening the multi-creased thing, my jaw dropped. "Where'd you get this?" It was a picture of Joanna Whitechapel, aka Desiree Luscious.

"It fell out of his wallet when he pulled out his valet ticket. He was in such a hurry to leave, he didn't even notice. I picked it up and saw who it was. I had to go lean against the side of the building until my legs stopped wobbling."

Once the guys caught up with us, I showed Corrigan the photograph. "Norm dropped this."

Corrigan studied it. "Looks like Norm is going to need an alibi."

Chapter Seventeen

Angie, Corrigan, Gino, Ed and I headed back inside Palacio's only to be stopped by Aunt Lena and Betty. They had been waiting for us at the maitre d stand.

My aunt practically shoved a white box with the restaurant's logo at me. "Here. You hardly touched your cannelloni so I had them wrap it up for you."

I opened my mouth to protest, but she interrupted, "You're welcome. It's not like you make so much money you can afford to leave food behind." She switched subjects like a racecar driver switches gears. "So, Angie, what happened? Did you two make up?"

Ed stepped in. "Lena, I got an early shift tomorrow. Why don't I fill you in on our way home?"

Betty hooked her arm through Gino's. "That sounds like a good idea. Gino, why don't we do the same?"

Both couples departed, leaving Angie and me with Corrigan, who was already on his phone about Norm. Meanwhile, Angie's shoulders slumped and she fidgeted with the tassel on her purse. When I tried to make eye contact with her, she looked away.

Corrigan finished his call. "We have his plate number and address so it won't be long before I'm talking to him again."

"Great. If you don't need us, Brian, I'm going to take Angie home."

"Did you valet park?"

"Of course. Doesn't every underemployed, barely squeaking-by woman toss her money on valet parking?"

He grinned. Then he offered to walk us to my car.

"It's not necessary." I pointed down the street. "We're right there."

"Okay then." Barely bushing my lips with his, Corrigan bade us goodnight.

We were halfway to her home and Angie hadn't said a word the whole way. "Are you okay?"

"Sure. Why wouldn't I be? I just got off a date with a killer, not only put myself in danger, but my best friend's niece." She shook her head and tsk'd. "How could I have been so foolish? You tried to warn me, but—"

"But nothing. I doubt there's anyone in the world that hasn't done something foolish in the name of romance."

She tugged on the bodice of her dress and muttered, "I'm old enough to know better. Who knows what would've happened to me if you hadn't insisted on coming along? Of course, the rest of the crowd…" She shook her head.

"Hey, my apologies about everyone showing up."

A deep sigh. "It's okay. Nobody died and that's a

good thing." As an afterthought she added, "At least nobody in our group."

I waited until she locked her front door behind her. Thinking that, like Angie, there'd be nobody waiting at home for me, a wave of wistfulness took me by surprise. Would someone, namely Corrigan, ever be anticipating my return home? As soon as my brain got wind of that sentiment, it tried to drown it in logic. There was no time for that feeling now. Now there was a serial killer to find and women to keep safe. I kept myself busy thinking those thoughts until I made it back to my apartment. Besides, I had Charlie and it was enough that he was waiting with licks and a wagging tail. And he wouldn't argue with me about my involvement in murder cases.

In fact, Charlie was probably happier to see me than most people. Or maybe he was just thrilled to see me take him for a walk. Reluctant as I was to go back outside, the poor pup had been cooped up for way too long. The leash went on Charlie and my gun on me. My phone came along, just in case.

We took our usual route, down to the cul-de-sac at the end of our street. There's a heavily treed field there which Charlie loves. Once we reached his favorite place, he pulled me to a stop twice. After the second time, I felt a shift in my surroundings. As if someone beside Charlie and me was now present. Confirming my senses, Charlie's ears pricked up and his tail lowered. He didn't go so far as to growl, but there was no friendliness in his stance. A twig snapped nearby and made my heart beat double-time. Panic flooded my brain, making it harder to think. I spun around but saw nothing out of the ordinary.

Another footstep. This one sounding closer. I twisted my head from side to side. Nobody there. At least no one I could see. I clutched my gun with my clammy, free hand just as Charlie yanked on his leash. He took off running and barking, jerking me along. Just as suddenly he halted and began sniffing at the grass while I almost flew over him before skidding to a stop. Catching my breath, I no longer sensed someone watching me. I began to wonder if it hadn't just been some animal. Still, I tugged on Charlie's leash to hurry him to my apartment. I didn't relax until I dead-bolted the door and then immediately double-checked it.

Corrigan was calling. I'd think about what happened during Charlie's walk later.

"Hey. Just want to make sure you're okay. You are, aren't you?"

"I am now." *Should I tell him about what I'd just felt outside?* I decided against it. He was tired and stretched to breaking. Plus, what would I say? That I felt somebody or something nearby? It could've been a raccoon. Or maybe it was Norm.

"Good." He yawned into the phone and apologized for doing so. "Before we hang up, I meant to tell you how great you looked tonight."

I was grinning like a simpleton, but nobody was there to see it but Charlie and he didn't pass judgment. "Thank you. You did too."

He chuckled softly. “Get some sleep. I’ll talk to you soon.”

“Love you.”

“Yeah, me too.”

My smile accompanied me all the way to the bedroom. But the minute my head touched the pillow, the memory of feeling spied upon hit me like a tsunami. I threw the covers aside and, after again checking all the windows and door, coaxed Charlie to join me in bed.

The next morning I woke up with Charlie’s head on my pillow. After I brushed his fur from my nose, I got up and turned on the television for the latest on the Red Bow Killer. But there was only a rehash of what was already known about the killer’s victims. Nothing about Norm as a person of interest, so after my morning Charlie-related duties, I took a shower. While eating an English muffin spread with Nutella, I decided since Sunday was my one day off, I’d spend it crime-solving.

I had just turned on my laptop when Gino called. With one action, the man could make my plans vaporize.

“Hi, Claire. Fine morning, isn’t it?”

“You’re in a good mood.”

“Ya know, I did get Norm the Worm—I just made that up—to break.” I could picture Gino puffing out his chest. “If he hadn’t bolted we wouldn’t have found the vic’s picture on him. That’s what a good PI does.”

Unbelievable! The man could spin even his buffoonery into an act of skill and cunning. “So the cops owe it all to you?”

"Nah, you did good dropping the hint that Norm would be at the restaurant with you. Great set-up."

The only thing stopping me from hanging up on Gino was reminding myself he was my boss. I settled for shaking my head and bursting his bubble. "Don't expect to collect the reward. Desiree was only one victim. Who knows? Maybe her death wasn't even related to Eileen's."

"You're thinking copycat? No way." But he didn't sound as confident.

We could have gone on like that all day, but I had research to do and Gino had…I didn't know what he had to do. I soon found out.

He blew out a breath. "Anyway, I figured it's time to get the word out about the agency."

Glad to hear the end to his bragging, I said, "That's a good idea. We could use more business."

"Do you think it's too early to advertise that I'm the one who took down the Red Bow Killer?"

In what reality did this guy live? "Yeah, much too early." I didn't add, 'and much too fabricated.'

"Hey, getting another call. Gotta go."

Giving my phone dirty looks as if it were the cause of my irritation, I returned to my laptop. Not for long. Gino called back.

"Claire! Just got off the phone with a friend of mine. Cops are questioning Norm Rockwell about all the murders. That fool hasn't got one single alibi." He chuckled, and I imagined him rubbing his hands together like the wicked witch in a fairy tale. "I smell reward money."

"What makes you think you'll get the reward money now?" Norm hadn't even been charged yet. Sure, he didn't have alibis for the nights of the murders, but they still needed motive and a way to tie him to the crimes.

"Don't worry, Claire. I'll split with you. A deal's a deal. Gotta tell Betty."

"Wait. Don't get her hopes up. Not yet anyway."

"You're right. She's a delicate flower, that woman."

While that description was far from accurate, I wasn't about to argue. Instead, I switched subjects. "Before it all shakes out, what about this advertising for new clients?"

The sound of him tapping his fingers against something hard accompanied his words. "You're right. Strike while the strikin's good. I'll pick up some business cards. Expect a whole bunch of new clients tomorrow."

Did I want to know how he was going to drum up this business? *No*. As soon as that conversation ended, I called Corrigan. Convinced I'd have to leave a message, I was surprised when he actually answered.

"Detective Corrigan here."

"Hi Brian." I used my sweetest voice. "I—"

He finished my sentence. "—wanted to know if we've arrested Rockwell. Not yet. After that fiasco with Gutkowski we want a solid case."

"So Norm's free?" Recalling last night's scary episode in the field, my throat tightened. Maybe now was the time to tell Corrigan. "Uh, what time did you bring him in for questioning?" My attempt to sound casual was thwarted by the dog-whistle pitch of my voice.

Suspicious, he said, "Not until this morning. Why?"

The story poured out of me like water out of a fountain.

"Why didn't you tell me this when I called last night?" I could almost feel his frustration through the phone.

I didn't want to argue with him, but felt like I had to explain. "I can take care of myself. Besides, you've already got your hands full doing your job."

He inhaled and blew out a deep breath. "Making sure you're safe is part of my job. Far as I'm concerned, the most important."

Those sweet words turned me cookie-batter soft. "I really appreciate that and you, Brian. But I don't even know if there was someone there or not. Maybe it was a raccoon or a squirrel." I didn't really believe that, but there was no sense in Corrigan feeling frustrated with me for a past event.

"Yeah, okay. But don't go out after dark by yourself."

"Fine. I'll tell Charlie to hold it until daylight."

"Yeah. Good point. Okay. Just stay by the building when you take him out."

This was getting us nowhere. "Do you really think Norm is the Red Bow Killer?"

"Doesn't matter what I think. It's whatever the evidence shows and so far it's showing him as the guy."

In the background I heard a voice. Corrigan apologized to me and with a quick goodbye, he hung up.

After going to Sunday mass, I spent the rest of the morning and afternoon trying to fathom Norm's motive for the murders. I couldn't come up with anything that made sense. True, he played a musical instrument and he liked bingo. He didn't seem to have any grudges against women who played bingo, though. Or did he just hide it well? I didn't get a chance to ask Corrigan what explanation Norm gave about Desiree's picture in his wallet. That certainly didn't scream innocence.

Digging into Norm's background, the only thing that stood out was that originally he was from Steubenville, Ohio. And Steubenville was only 45 minutes from Pittsburgh, where all those murders a decade ago took place. He looked to be in his mid-to-late fifties so he could have been killing women ten years ago. Maybe even ten years before that. But why wait ten years? What happened to make him stop and what triggered him to start again?

My phone interrupted my thoughts-that-led-nowhere. It was Suzy, Dad's fiancé, soon to be my stepmother, although I doubted she'd want me to call her Mom.

"Hi Claire. Whatcha doing?"

"Trying to solve a murder."

Suzy giggled as if I were joking. "If you're not busy tonight stomping out crime, could you come for dinner?"

The invitation put a smile on my face. "I'm free. What time?" Not only would I get to see my father and

Suzy, but I wouldn't be scrounging for food. Even if Charlie couldn't come with me since my dad was allergic to dogs, my pup could still perhaps enjoy a bit of leftovers.

After giving me what time dinner was, we chitchatted a little longer. Then we said our goodbyes.

The rest of the day passed without any calamity, which, given what had been happening lately, was a relief. A quiet afternoon. Just Charlie, my laptop, and me.

My stomach was growling by the time I pulled into my father's driveway. I knocked on the door and let myself in. The delicious aroma of chicken, lemon, and oregano whispered loving thoughts to my stomach.

My father was standing over a wooden salad bowl. He was wearing a black and white striped chef's apron that said, "Don't complain to me, I'm just the sous chef."

He gave me a hug and handed me a slice of cucumber. "Suzy's freshening up. She says I don't need to; I'm fresh enough." He chuckled while I groaned.

Ever since he and Suzy became an item, Dad seemed ten years younger. A happy man. Nonna used to tell me that a loved man is a long-lived man. I hoped she was right. Of course, she also used to say marriage took five years off a woman's life and fifteen years off her looks.

Suzy, fixing her non-existent stray hairs, entered the kitchen. Her apron said, "Any complaints will be handled by the sous chef." While we hugged, my father disappeared and returned with a bottle of Prosecco. He poured each of us a glass and Suzy made the toast. “To Claire, who I hope will agree to be my maid of honor.”

My lips curved into a smile. “I would love to!”

She embraced me, careful not to spill the wine, and we giggled as if we were 17 and gabbing about the senior prom.

As my dad removed the fragrant browned chicken from the oven, we chatted about the wedding plans. Since it was going to be a simple ceremony, there would just be a best man to match the maid of honor. My father wasn’t sure yet who he would choose.

The next day they had appointments at three different venues. Then it’d be ordering the cake, the flowers, and choosing a caterer.

“Aren’t you going to ask Aunt Lena to cater?”

Dad and Suzy looked at each other. My dad cleared his throat. “We’re still discussing that.”

I probed no further.

Dinner and my companions were a delight. By the end of the evening my affection for them softened the edges of everything, practically giving the world a glow. I’ve adored my dad since the first time he lowered me onto a tricycle. Now I was sharing him with Suzy, but instead of that love being divided, it doubled.

After dinner we told stories about each other and laughed until Suzy grabbed her sides and begged us to stop. That’s when I checked the time and realized I’d stayed much later than I’d planned.

With a plate of leftovers in hand, I expressed my

gratitude. My dad walked me to my car, opened the door for me, and said, "Thank you, Pumpkin." When I gave him a questioning look, he explained. "You and Suzy are the most precious people in the world to me, and you've welcomed her into our family with open arms. Your mother raised you right."

I hate to be a sentimental softy, but my eyes filled. "You both did. Suzy's wonderful, Dad. Cherish each other."

"Hey, that's the kind of advice a father gives his daughter on her wedding day."

Grimacing, I joked, "By the time that happens, I'll be too hard of hearing for you to bother."

"No. I bet Brian will—"

"No. Brian may not." That denial made me so sad. I was shocked. "I better go. Love you, Dad."

All the way home I thought about whether Brian would or wouldn't. I loved him and he loved me. But sometimes I was afraid our feelings would get covered in the sludge we threw at each other pursuing our individual careers.

Finally home, I unlocked my apartment door to the sounds of Charlie's happy grunts and whimpers. Remembering last night's frightening experience, I nonetheless picked up his leash, along with my gun, and we headed outside. This time, though, we'd stay close by the apartment.

Chapter Eighteen

Charlie had done his business by a bush near the apartment. After giving him a few 'good boys,' we turned and strode up the walkway. A squirrel audaciously popped in front of Charlie and then dashed toward the field at the end of the street. My dog took off after the fluffy-tailed rodent and, in so doing, ripped the leash from my hand. I rubbed my scraped palm with my other hand and ran after the duo, calling Charlie's name.

Upon reaching the edge of the field, I skidded to a stop. There was Charlie, munching on a patch of something. Leaning over, I grabbed onto the leash and began scolding my runaway pet. We turned in the direction of the apartment building. That's when Charlie began growling.

There was one lonely street light and I glimpsed what I thought was someone's shadow. My body tensed. Though my heart was pounding out a beat no drummer could keep up with, I didn't run. My free hand on my gun, I called out, "Who's there?"

Nothing.

I shouted again, "Who's there?"

Charlie went from a growl to barking and straining at the leash. I whispered, "Take me to him, boy." And let the leash go. He took off and I followed. All the way to the apartment, where Charlie stopped.

Whoever had been watching me was now gone. Along with my courage. As the adrenaline rush subsided, my legs were like melted plastic and my hands trembled so hard it was difficult to unlock my apartment door.

The previous night had been scary. Tonight was downright heart-attack producing. Last night Shadow Man stayed at a distance. Tonight he came much closer. I shivered. There wouldn't be a tomorrow night.

When my hands stopped shaking enough, I filled Charlie's water bowl and called Corrigan. He couldn't accuse me of holding back this time. Of course, he didn't pick up. Pacing, I recapped what had just happened into voicemail.

Although it was late, I knew there would be no sleep for me for a while, if at all. So a diet pop, the television remote, and Charlie all joined me on the sofa.

***

My alarm sounded off in the distance that next morning. I rubbed my eyes, slowly waking up and realizing I'd slept on the sofa. The last thing I remembered was watching an old episode of *Friends*. Gently sweeping Charlie off my lap, I stumbled into the bedroom and turned off the clock. That's when I realized my phone had been ringing.

It was Corrigan. "Are you all right?"

Last night's scare rolled over me with the force of a bowling ball hitting the pins. Upon finding my voice, I whined, "It took you long enough to check on me." I grimaced, realizing my tone resembled that of a nagging wife's. *Feeling neglected, or plain scared?*

"Sorry, but I didn't get a chance to even check messages until just before I called you."

The tone of his voice was so deplete of hope, I had to ask, "I'm sorry. What happened last night? Was someone else killed?"

It took him a moment to respond. "Yeah."

My mouth felt so dry I could've used Charlie's water bowl. "Where?"

"This is still hush-hush so you didn't hear it from me. Body was found on Clifton. Near Lakewood Park."

This time the killer hit much closer to my home. My stomach clenched as I recalled last night's shadow. Did Charlie scare the killer away from me and toward another?

Corrigan must have thought the same thing. "I don't want you going out alone at night. At all. The dog will just have to use papers until we put Norm Rockwell away."

Trying to disguise the terror I was feeling, I went for humor. "So until he paints himself in a corner?"

Corrigan either didn't get my feeble joke about Norm's famous namesake or chose to ignore it. "We had a tail on him, but those morons lost him after the anniversary party where he was playing. They didn't pick up his scent again until an hour and a half later."

"The woman was killed during the time he was MIA?"

"We just have an approximate time of death. But it's close enough to bring Rockwell in. With some luck, he'll never see the light of day again. Still, I mean what I said about going out alone. Not until they throw the key away on the bastard."

I grabbed at the only straw I knew. "What if it isn't him?"

"What? It's gotta be." Corrigan's patience was thinning quickly. "Why would he have disappeared just at that time? Plus, that party was a perfect location. It was at the Roman Room. He could easily have done the murder, dumped her body, and let himself be found in that amount of time."

My tone sharper than I'd meant, I said, "Listen, I hope you're right. The whole city hopes you're right. And if you are, I'm really proud of you. Right now, though, I have to get ready for work."

"My turn to apologize. I'm like a live grenade. If we have the right guy I'll take you out to any place you want to go. Love you."

"Me too." I didn't bother to think about what place to choose until there was no doubt of Norm's guilt.

I showered, dressed and downed a Pop-Tart in twenty-two minutes, took Charlie outside, and was in my car in another fifteen. Had I known what was waiting for me at Gino's office, I would've taken some aspirins with me.

Chapter Nineteen

There was a line of people waiting to see Gino. All with so-called important cases they wanted solved. Since Gino wasn't in, the first woman settled for me after I assured her I was also a PI. Bobbie Hathaway was her name. She was in medical scrubs and wore the sour expression of someone assigned bedpan duty.

"I'm Claire DeNardo, Private Investigator. What can the Francini Agency help you with?"

Her expression changed from sour to irate, with her face reddening and her eyes narrowing. "I want you to find out who's stealing my lunch from the office refrigerator. I get so mad just thinking of it."

My hands lifted off the keyboard. "Someone's stealing your lunches and you want us to find the thief?"

"That's what I said. You deaf?"

"No. It's just that I'm not sure you need us for that situation." I was trying to be diplomatic.

She harrumphed. "Well, the guy handing me this," She showed me Gino's business card. "Told me no problem was too small."

This was his idea of drumming up business? I plastered a bland smile on my face. "Well then, let's get started. When was the last time you saw your lunch?"

Our intake completed, I confessed to Ms. Hathaway that Gino himself would have to determine the fee for this job.

"That's okay by me. Long as it's not over $50."

I stifled a laugh. "You'll hear from him as soon as he returns to the office."

The next client, a man with the misfortune to be named B.A. Dodor, sulked toward my desk. "Wanna hire this guy," also showing me Gino's card, "to find out who's been writing BAD Odor all over my locker, my toolbox, everything at work."

Rubbing my forehead to fight off a headache, I took down his information and gave him the same spiel about the fee.

Unlike Ms. Hathaway, Mr. Dodor replied, "I don't care what it costs. I want that sonofabitch caught. I'll take it from there."

Gino's voice carried from the hallway. "Excuse me." He was evidently trying to get through the waiting crowd. When he reached my desk, he stopped and I introduced Gino to Mr. Dodor. Gino shook his hand. "Nice to meet you, but would you excuse us for a second?"

"No problem. I'm done anyway. Get back to me soon. Somebody's gonna be real sorry they messed with my name."

To my surprise, Gino walked out to the crowd and announced, "The office is closed for break time. Please come back in an hour."

Some woman yelled, "Offices don't close for break time."

A guy muttered, "Don't expect me to come back."

Gino closed the door on them. "They arrested Rockwell. Sounds like the case is solid. The last victim was killed during the time the cops lost him. Oh, her name was Pam Jaworsky and, guess what?" He answered before I could open my mouth. "She was fond of bingo."

Gino was rambling on about the reward, but I was preoccupied with wanting to make two calls. The first to Corrigan to verify Gino's information. The second to Angie to make sure she was all right.

Corrigan answered on the first ring. He sounded as elated as a school kid on a snow day. "We got him, Claire."

"I heard. Congratulations." My voice wasn't exactly booming with enthusiasm, so I tried harder. "You must feel great about it."

"Yeah. Captain's off my back so I feel 190 pounds lighter. I've got paperwork to do, but how about I take you to lunch?"

"That would be wonderful." If I couldn't get excited about believing Norm was the Red Bow Killer, I could about seeing Corrigan his usual cocky self again.

"I'll pick you up at your office at noon. Is Frankie &

Johnny's good for you?"

A vision of their chocolate derby pie flashed through my mind, lighting up all the circuits. "Perfect."

My next call was to Angie. She'd find out about Norm anyway. I'd rather she got it from me first. Not that I thought she'd be devastated, but if it weren't for her mistaking him for a good guy and agreeing to dinner, Norm might never have been caught. She deserved thanks.

Angie answered her phone and after our greetings I broke the news to her.

She responded with, "Oh dear God. I really know how to pick them. Sixteen years without a date and the first man I go out with is a serial killer." Her voice thickened. "Didn't they make a movie like this?"

"He seemed sweet, Angie. You couldn't have known. And if it hadn't been for you finding the victim's photo, he might never have been caught."

She sighed, "But I was so nasty to everyone at dinner…"

I chuckled, "I would have been worse in your position. If it was Aunt Lena instead of you, imagine how unpleasant *she* would have been."

This got her laughing. "Good point." She paused then asked, "I was going to bingo tonight at Corey's Bingo Center. Since it's your night off from *Cannoli's*, would you like to come with me? It's more fun going with somebody."

My nose wrinkled, but I owed her. "Sure. I can meet

you there. What time?"

We were saying our goodbyes when Gino stepped out of his office and opened the door to the hallway. "The crowd's building again."

I groaned and got up to escort the first of these new clients to my desk.

It was a long morning, but finally noon rolled around. Corrigan showed up right on time. Since Gino had already left for lunch, I locked up.

For the first time since the Red Bow murders began, Corrigan looked refreshed. His grin was infectious and I responded in kind. Too bad I didn't have dimples like his.

After he kissed me hello I said, "You look happier than I've seen you in a while. I was getting worried about you."

He opened the car door for me. "Appreciate the concern. It's just that it's taken so long to get this killer locked up."

"I hope he turns out to be the right guy." Wrong thing to say.

The vein in Corrigan's temple throbbed. "He's the right guy, all right." Counting on his fingers, he said, "One, a neighbor of Joanna Whitechapel, or Desiree, claims she saw him hanging around the victim's home. Two, the guy slipped out just in time to kill the latest victim, Pam Jaworsky. And three, no alibis for any of the murders. Yeah, we got the right guy."

Rather than continue with an argument guaranteed to

irritate him, I switched topics and described some of Gino's new cases. It was a successful ploy. By the time we arrived at the restaurant, we were both loosened up and were having a good time.

For lunch I had a diet pop and the chocolate derby pie, oozing with chocolate and walnuts. He had a reuben sandwich with fries and a chocolate shake. I promised myself I'd have a granola bar for dinner to balance out the calories in the pie. With a flash of jealousy, I realized he'd probably have a full dinner and not put on an ounce. That uncharitable feeling was swiftly replaced with sympathy. The poor guy had probably existed on coffee, stale pastries, and takeout Chinese for the past week or so.

I reached out and gently cradled his cheek in my hand. He turned his face slightly and kissed my palm. My insides melted like the wax of a lit candle. But nothing could come of the sparks that flew between us. At least not now, since we both had to get back to work. He must have been thinking the same thing, because a slow, regretful smile spread across his face.

On the way back to my office, I let it slip that I was going to play bingo that night with Angie. Corrigan chortled, "Careful, you play enough of that and it could be a gateway to other types of gambling. Shooting craps in a smoky backroom, poker with a bunch of sweaty t-shirted men—"

"I don't know. I thought cockfights might be more my style."

He looked about to say something. Then must have thought better of it. Instead he grew serious. "Be careful. I mean, we've got the Red Bow Killer, but you never know if there's some wacko copycat."

I patted his shoulder. "Angie and I will be fine." The truth was, I didn't fear a copycat killer but the real deal. A nagging suspicion kept popping into my head that arresting Norm wasn't the end of the story. Rather than tell Corrigan that, though, I kept it to myself and continued keeping the peace. Why get him angry or frustrated or whatever emotion my doubt would produce?

Corrigan walked me to the door of Francini's Agency. An older, dark-haired man, a walking stick in his hand, turned toward Corrigan and me. "Are either of you Private Investigator Francini?"

Corrigan murmured, "Thank God, no."

I shot him a censoring look and then answered, "Sorry, Mr. Francini isn't in yet. I'm his assistant. Can I help you?"

I said my farewells to Corrigan, then invited the fellow into the office and offered him a chair.

The gentleman interlaced his fingers and stretched them as if he was going to play a keyboard. He cleared his throat. "My name is Joseph Griselli."

When he didn't continue, I leaned toward him, "And how can the Francini Agency help you?" I was sure he wanted Gino to do something like finding his lost pet parakeet.

He opened and closed his mouth twice, as if the

words sat on the tip of his tongue but refused to take the final leap out. My foot began tapping as if keeping the beat of an unheard tune.

With a deep breath, he finally began, "I've come here from Pittsburgh."

That caught my attention. I asked the next question, but my gut already knew the answer. "You were living there a decade ago when those twelve women were murdered?"

When he nodded, the hairs on my arms rose. "And that's why you're here?"

He ran his fingers through his sparse gray hair. "After I went to Eileen's funeral, I met up with a mutual acquaintance who recommended you."

He stared beyond me. "Eileen and me were an item ten years back. At least until she found someone else, a musician. It was hard, but I settled for being her friend. She disappeared right after the guy accused of those murders hanged himself."

"Did you ever meet her boyfriend?"

"No. She kept him under wraps. I don't know. Maybe she was embarrassed, or the guy was the jealous type."

Poised at the edge of my seat, I asked, "Did she at least tell you his name?"

He shrugged his broad shoulders. "Just called him 'Music Man' all the time because he played in some two-bit rock band. But she did let it slip that he wasn't originally from Pittsburgh. Came from Ohio."

My mouth felt so dry cacti could've grown in it. "Was it Steubenville, Ohio?"

"Might've been. But by the time Eileen started seeing him he already lived in Pittsburgh. She told me one time about how, when he was moving here, some of his furniture slid down the hill."

I bit the corner of my lower lip and wondered if Norm Rockwell had resided in Pittsburgh yet had somehow stayed under the radar.

"What is it you want from our agency?"

"The person who murdered Eileen." He tapped the end of his cane on the floor. "I'd lay money this 'Music Man' and her killer are the same guy."

"After ten years? Why now? You think it took him this long to find her?"

"It did me."

Gino chose that time to return. He practically ignored me and stuck his hand out to Griselli. "I'm Gino Francini, owner of this agency. How can I help you?"

Griselli nodded to me and I repeated his story.

For once, Gino didn't interrupt. When I was done he shook his head and murmured, "I'll be damned."

Since Gino didn't ask any questions, I wondered aloud if Timothy, whom I assumed Griselli meant by a mutual friend, was surprised when Griselli introduced himself.

"Didn't talk to the guy. I went to pay my respects to Eileen." Griselli's shoulders drooped a bit. "She was a real special lady."

Pursuing the question of what Timothy knew, I asked, "Do you think she would have told her brother about you?"

Griselli clasped his hands together. "Eileen and me knew each other a long time ago, but even then she was secretive, kept things to herself."

"Mr. Griselli, you *are* aware Norm Rockwell has already been arrested and charged with Eileen's murder. Aren't you?"

"Yeah. Well, if this Rockwell guy really did kill Eileen, I want you to make sure there's enough evidence that he hangs. If somebody else is the killer, though, find him."

The wheels in Gino's mind were obviously spinning. "But the cops already have enough proof to arrest and hold Rockwell."

"Pfft. You call what they have enough? I gotta be sure." Griselli lowered his chin and his scowl told me he'd planned on meting out justice to Eileen's murderer himself. He'd just been too late to get at Norm.

I was worried if we didn't agree to his request, Griselli would find someone who would. Still, I had to be positive we were aiming for the same final result. "Any evidence we find supporting Norm Rockwell as the killer, as well as if he's not and we find the real killer, gets turned over to the police."

Gino's eyes narrowed and he gave an almost imperceptible nod, as if he only just now understood. "We don't get involved in any vigilante activity. I have to insist that any information, including what you've just told us, be passed to the authorities."

I wondered if an invisible ventriloquist had worked Gino's mouth, declaring he'd play this one straight.

It seemed Griselli was taken aback too. The men took stock of each other and to my amazement, our client caved. "Okay. We'll play it your way."

I could only hope he'd be true to his words.

After a quick moment, Griselli added, "But my name stays out of any information that goes to the cops. The boys-in-blue and I've never seen eye-to-eye."

I objected, "But surely, in this case—"

He talked over me. "Going to them might cause me an unwanted incarceration. So I'm not involved in this. Understand?"

Gino tapped his temple with his index finger as if that would shift an idea from his brain to his tongue. "You could disappear first. Then I'll tell the cops what you said."

"Yeah? I don't think so."

Out of desperation, I offered an alternate plan. "I could go see the detective on the case." Before Griselli could object, I added to the idea. "You could write a note, or better yet, type it and include what you've told us. It doesn't have to mention who you are. I'll present it to the police as an anonymous tip. Meanwhile, Gino and I will continue working on the assignment so the police definitely have the right guy in jail."

Griselli leaned against his cane and for a moment, I

feared he'd get up and walk out on us. Instead he said, "As long as my name stays out of everything, you got a deal." Pulling out a roll of bills so big it resembled a green log, he added, "I have the first half of a nice fee for both of you." Griselli peeled off the hefty sum of $4,000 as a down payment. All in cash. The ease with which he parted from the bills made me wonder if they were counterfeit.

He glanced at the office walls. "Maybe you could use it to spruce up this place."

Gino looked offended but didn't say anything. To ensure he didn't get the chance, I sprang from my chair. "Here, Mr. Griselli. Use my computer for your statement."

It took him a while as he pecked at the keyboard with two meaty fingers, but Griselli finally finished and asked me to read his statement. It included living in Pittsburgh when the women were murdered, his affair with Eileen, and her relationship with a guy in a rock band she'd referred to as 'Music Man.' He ended with what he'd told us about the musician's previous residence. I printed the note, folded it, and placed it in my purse.

The question I'd been dying to ask pushed through my lips. "Now that we're working together, Mr. Griselli, who is the mutual friend?"

One corner of his mouth turned up. "Guy from New Jersey. He couldn't get involved, but he recommended you. Said, pardon the expression, you had balls."

My heart almost stopped. He had to mean Michael Bucanetti, the mob boss who pulled a lot of strings in Cleveland. I'd had a number of experiences with him, most of them life-threatening.

I must have looked as if I'd seen a tombstone with my name on it because Griselli held up his hands. "Like I said, he's not a part of this."

My breathing relaxed a bit but not completely. From experience, I knew Bucanetti could change his mind and become a part of this. I forced that concern from my mind, and we struck a deal.

As soon as Griselli left with a promise he'd be in touch, Gino closed the door behind him. "How the hell are we going to pull this off?"

"You mean giving the police Griselli's statement but not telling them who he is?"

He frowned and waved his hand. "No. Convincing Griselli that Norm *is* the killer. Otherwise, we'll have to find the real killer and even the cops couldn't do that."

I pressed my lips together so as not to argue with my boss. But the urge was too strong. "I keep saying it, but nobody listens. There's a possibility, however remote, that Norm isn't guilty. Yes, he lived in a small city in Ohio, but there's no proof he ever moved to Pittsburgh. Plus, the night we met Norm, he claimed he'd never played in a rock band like 'Music Man' did. He'd have no reason to lie to us about that. We need to explore further."

Giving me an impatient look, Gino said, "What are

you? Christopher Columbus? There's no need to explore. Norm is the Red Bow Killer. Period. End of story."

"Next you'll tell me the world's flat and I'll fall off if I keep going." I grabbed the note Griselli had just written. "I'm taking this to the police." My hand on the doorknob, I added, "The guy who recommended us is Michael Bucanetti. If we don't play this straight, we might not live to spend Griselli's money."

I hated to throw Bucanetti's name around, but it did the trick. Gino's jaw dropped and he didn't offer any rebuttal.

Chapter Twenty

Corrigan wasn't at the police station. Another detective offered to take the note but I insisted on giving it only to Corrigan. The cop shrugged, "Suit yourself. Don't know when he'll be back though."

My decision to wait a while was smart. Getting a cup of coffee thick as mud from the vending machine wasn't. I had just returned from the restroom where I scrubbed the sludge off my teeth with a paper towel when Corrigan returned.

He escorted me to his desk. "Lunch with you was pure pleasure. By your expression, this must be business."

"Yes, seeing you this afternoon was wonderful. You're right, though. This is business." I waved Griselli's note in front of Corrigan as I had previously done with Rose's.

His eyes followed the folded piece of paper. "Rose sent Betty another note?"

Now was the time I'd find out how good my acting

skills were. "No. Someone slipped this under the agency's door after the guy you saw with the cane left. I heard a noise and went to investigate. All I found was that." I nodded toward the paper.

He pulled out a pair of latex gloves from his desk and took the note skimming through it. "And you didn't see anyone around?"

Keeping my voice level with just a hint of puzzlement, I responded, "No."

This time he took longer to go through the note. "You know it doesn't mean Norm isn't the killer."

I held my tongue, but my expression must have given me away.

With a deep, patience-seeking breath, Corrigan asked, "Why is it so hard for you to believe Norm's our man?"

Sitting across from him, I squinted, wanting to force my thoughts into his brain. Yeah, like that was going to work. So I stewed rather than answer him.

He leaned toward me. "The author of this note didn't bother coming forward. This information could have been written by some crackpot getting his jollies."

"But—"

The look he gave me was similar to my dad's whenever, as a teen, I argued that he should allow me to have the car any time I wanted it. The look said, no way, as clearly as any words.

"I'll enter this into the case file. If you find out who wrote it, I'll question them. But without knowing if this is legitimate or not, there's not much I can do."

I nodded, mumbling just below hearing level, "Or want to do."

Knowing I was upset, he gently teased, "We'll both feel better when this case is over. I'm due for some time off and my plan is to spend as much of it with you as you'll let me."

In spite of my frustration, my lips curved upwards. "Be careful what you wish for."

While he was chuckling, I took my leave, feeling very much alone in this case.

By the time I got back to the office, Gino was preparing to leave. "Got some running around to do. I'll grab a late lunch. From there I thought I'd see who's maligning B.A. Odor's name." He chortled, "Guy needs to change his moniker."

Closing the door behind him he said, "Probably won't be back until tomorrow."

It was already three and, having done no office work all day, I picked up reports to file. After a whole five minutes, I dropped the papers and began working on my computer. Forty minutes of that was all I could stand.

Bingo at Corey's Center began at six. If I left work right then, I'd have enough time to feed and walk Charlie, eat something myself, and meet Angie before the first game. I closed my computer down, grabbed my purse, and was out the door by a quarter after four.

***

Charlie was fed, watered and walked and I had

downed two granola bars and a diet pop by five thirty. Not having to speed to get to Corey's allowed me to relax and be in a decent frame of mind when Angie and I met up.

She, on the other hand, was wearing a scowl mean enough to keep even the most intrepid bingo players from sitting at our table.

"What's wrong, Angie?"

"Your aunt. She signed me up for some over-50 dating site called, Plenty of Life." Angie fumed. "As if I'm so desperate, I need a computer to find me a man." She crossed her arms. "She kept bringing up Norm. I choose one serial killer..."

I placed my hand on her shoulder. "Don't let Aunt Lena get to you. She means well. She just doesn't always go about things the right way."

Angie rubbed her forehead. "Yeah. You're right. It's just...Oh, never mind." She took in a deep breath and blew it out. "Okay, let's play bingo."

The first game went by quickly, with a man in a wheelchair I'd never seen before as the winner. While he and the host reviewed the numbers, Jerry, the old gentleman from Smalley's Chocolates and other bingo games, shuffled in. Moving at the speed of a snail, he made his way to the table closest to the entrance and sat.

The second game had just begun when we heard a thump. Someone screamed, "Help! Help! Call 911!"

I spun around and saw Jerry, face down on the table. A woman claiming to be a nurse rushed over to him and checked his pulse. He was alive but not breathing. Just as Angie and I, plus two others, helped get him to the floor so the nurse could begin compressions, Jerry opened his eyes. The nurse asked him his name, but he was pretty disoriented and seemed unable to speak. He pointed to his pocket and the woman removed his wallet. His Medicare card identified him as Gerald Wolden. *Not Malden as Angie had told me earlier.*

After the EMTs whisked Jerry away in an ambulance, bingo resumed. But many of the participants, shaken by what had just transpired, couldn't concentrate. There was so much conversation it was difficult to hear the host announce the numbers.

When eventually someone yelled that they had bingo, Angie nudged me. "Sorry I got Jerry's name wrong. Guess I'm not much of a detective."

"Don't worry about it." I couldn't be upset with her. She'd done her best and I couldn't even retrieve the memory of where I'd heard the name, Wolden, before. *Some detective I was.*

Not long after her apology, Angie tapped me on the shoulder, saying she'd lost interest in that night's game. She was going to call her son to pick her up. Just as well, because I was unable to focus either. Jerry's last name kept rolling around in my head, sort of like those metal balls in a pinball machine. Too bad it couldn't find a hole to fit in.

Chapter Twenty-One

I'd sound so dedicated if I claimed to have spent the rest of the night delving into the mystery of Jerry's name. I didn't. Instead, after playing with Charlie and walking him, I fell asleep and Monday slid into Tuesday morning.

As soon as I awoke, I checked the news and was relieved to learn it had been a serial-killer-free night. I turned off the television and after my morning preparations, went into work.

Ten minutes after I set my purse on my office desk, Gino called in, claiming he was going to spend the morning with Timothy. "We're gonna grab some breakfast and talk, you know, 'man-o-a-man-o.'"

Where does he come up with these expressions? "Have you heard anything new about Norm or the case against him?"

"Nope. Just what you already know." He paused. "Hey, we may get some more new clients today. Handle them with care, okay?"

In a voice sweet enough to cause tooth decay, I said,

"Clients will be treated super-duper special."

He harrumphed and hung up. After that, the day passed uneventfully, a refreshing change.

***

My evening at *Cannoli's* was a different story. Entering the kitchen, I heard Angie and my aunt having what is politely called, 'words.'

As soon as Aunt Lena spotted me, she drew me into the conversation. "Claire, tell Angie she shouldn't be meeting men at those gambling places."

Before I could refuse to get involved, Angie, through gritted teeth, responded. "Bingo isn't like going to the racetrack and picking up men."

My aunt folded her arms across her immense chest. "Um-hmm. I bet you wouldn't meet a serial killer on Plenty of Life."

Angie countered, "How do you know that, Lena? Have you met all the men on that computer site?"

I threw up my hands. "Stop! Aunt Lena, it's Angie's decision whether or not to use a dating site." My aunt held up her index finger to argue, but I went on, "Angie, I know you don't want any part of online dating, but you could look at the guys on it. Maybe you'll be pleasantly surprised."

Never one to let someone else have the last word, Aunt Lena nodded, "I just wanted to help, but Claire's right. It's your choice but I *did* sign you up for three months."

Angie's eyes opened wide and I was sure she'd lose

what composure she had. Happily, I was wrong. "Okay. I'll take a look tomorrow. Just so you know, though, that doesn't mean I'll go out with anyone."

By the sniff my aunt released, I knew she wasn't completely satisfied. Still, to my relief and no doubt Angie's, she dropped the topic and we bustled through the evening.

***

By Wednesday morning, I'd convinced myself Norm had to be the Red Bow Killer. After all, there had been bingo games held throughout the city and no new murders had occurred since his arrest. I was finally willing to admit they'd stopped because the murderer, Norm, was now incarcerated. The women of Cleveland, including me, could feel safer now. That was something in which to be grateful.

On that same day, Gino appeared in the office for only an hour, then disappeared until late in the afternoon. Just as well because once he learned the reward for finding Eileen's murderer was for the arrest *and* conviction, all he did was sulk. If he were to collect the $10,000 at all it wouldn't be right away.

"I had that money practically spent." Gino's eyes glossed over each time he talked about the money. The final time he mentioned it he added, "That's minus, of course, your share, Claire."

"Of course." I dropped the sarcasm from my voice and changed the subject. "I was thinking about Joseph Griselli. We need to dig up some evidence." At which point, the office phone rang. It was the very person we'd been discussing, Griselli.

Gino made for the exit. "Say I'm not here."

Instead of sticking my foot out to trip him, I chose to answer the phone, identifying myself. "What can I do for you, Mr. Griselli?"

"I want to cancel our agreement."

Shocked, I almost dropped the phone. Recovering quickly, I said in my most solicitous voice, "Can you tell me why?"

"Something came up."

When I realized that was all he was going to say, I prompted, "You won't change your mind?"

He huffed, "Not a chance. When can I come get my money?"

I glanced around as if expecting Gino to materialize. My voice weak, I explained, "I can't authorize the refund and my boss is out of the office."

"That so? When will he be in?" His tone shifted and became rougher, more threatening.

Having no idea as to the answer but not wanting to admit it, I said, "I'll contact him and explain the situation. Then get back to you as swiftly as possible."

"Deal. But it'll be in everyone's best interest if you don't keep me waiting long."

As soon as we hung up, I called Gino. Not surprisingly, it went right into his voicemail. Visions of a furious Griselli attacking me with his cane appeared in my mind's eye. If answering the phones and manning the office hadn't been the job that kept a roof over my head, I would've taken off. Instead, I checked my gun and nervously paced until Gino returned my call twenty minutes later. Too bad his instructions set off alarms in my head. "Set up an appointment with him for next Thursday."

I scrunched up my face. "There's nothing on the calendar between now and then. It's only right we…"

Gino blew out a deep breath. "Don't have the money. If we wait, we could get more business."

"How many stolen lunch investigations do we need for us to make up that amount of money?"

"Not funny, Claire. Make it next Thursday afternoon. See you later." He hung up before I could say another word.

A wormy feeling settled in my gut. Although I hated to lose any part of the fee that might have come my way, it was only right, and a lot safer for me, that the guy got his money back. Sooner than a week after he'd requested it. After all, we'd done nothing on the case yet.

Ready to risk losing my job for defying Gino's instructions, I called Griselli back. That he didn't answer his phone dampened the righteous fire in my heart and I had no choice but to leave a message asking he return my call.

By late afternoon Griselli hadn't called back. Rather than dwell on his situation, I switched to wondering about my own, namely, whether I should cancel my saxophone lessons. After all, if Norm was indeed the Red

Bow Killer did I really need to spend my scant supply of time and money learning to play an instrument?

On the plus side of continuing with the lesson was Aunt Lena being under the impression I was taking saxophone lessons to play at my dad's wedding and so didn't complain about time taken off. In addition, if I really pressured Gino, he might agree to pay some of the lesson fees. Minus side was no time, talent or desire to play. I made up my mind to cancel with Todd.

Then he called me to confirm and I couldn't bear to douse his sunshine with my dark thoughts about quitting before I'd really started. When I got off the phone I berated myself for being a softy. Trying to be optimistic, I told myself if I gave it a chance, it was possible I'd enjoy learning an instrument. I chuckled to myself. Maybe I'd get so good at it my dad would ask me to play the wedding processional as Suzy glided down the aisle.

Pulling myself from the reverie, I called Griselli again. Again, I left a message for him to call.

Chapter Twenty-Two

I arrived at Todd's store and studio ready to rock out on the sax. Since I was a bit early, I watched Todd instructing a young boy on the piano. His intensity in working with the child was such that he didn't notice me enter the room.

The boy, though, looked up and grinned at me as if grateful for the interruption. I excused myself and was ready to wait outside when Todd jumped up from the piano bench. "Jack and I are just about done. Please. Have a seat." He pointed to a chair on the other side of the small room.

Nodding and smiling at the boy, I took the offered chair and set my father's saxophone next to me.

After the boy left, Todd apologized. "There's been a family emergency, so I'm a bit behind. But I didn't want to postpone your lesson." He quickly added, "Since it's your first time."

My grin probably resembled the one I wore the first time a boy called me pretty. I glanced down. "I hope you won't regret it." Remembering my manners, I asked, "Is everything okay with your family now?"

"Yes. Thanks for asking. A close relative had a serious heart attack. He's better, but still in the hospital. I've been running back and forth. He doesn't have anyone else."

"So sorry. That must be tough."

He put on a brave face. "We make the best of things." He clapped his hands together. "Let's get started."

The lesson was painful. To his ears and my ego. By the end of the first thirty minutes, it was evident I hadn't inherited any musical ability from my father. To Todd's credit, he never grimaced once. Although I do think I noticed a half-hidden wince.

By the end of my allotted hour, red-faced and tired, I admitted defeat.

Todd shook his head. "You may find it hard to believe, but that wasn't bad for a beginner. Why don't you try one more lesson?" He flashed a smile that could charm a turtle out of her shell. "Then if you feel that you never want to touch the sax again, we'll call it quits."

As if someone had taken over the connection from my brain to my mouth, I said, "All right. One more."

He'd had a cancellation on Tuesday, so moved me up to that date. As I was leaving, he promised the lesson would begin on time. "Everything should be back to normal by then and I can turn my full attention to you." Almost as an afterthought he added, "And your saxophone." He closed his notebook. "Now I better lock up and get to the hospital. I'll walk you out."

Getting into my car, I had a feeling Todd Shotswell was interested in more than my ability to play the sax. It wasn't what he said as much as his body language. I twisted in my seat, feeling a bit guilty. I hadn't led him on. In fact, if he ever learned why I'd come to him in the first place, he wouldn't be so eager to teach me anything.

Hoping he'd sooth my prickly soul, I called Corrigan. When he answered his phone, he gave no indication he'd be up to the task.

"Claire, sorry but unless you can find a hole in a witness's statement, I can't talk right now."

My self-incrimination vanished, replaced by uneasiness. "Your case against Norm isn't as strong as you thought?"

"Let's talk about it tomorrow. Assuming I'm still alive after the Captain takes it out on my hide."

After our conversation ended, I sat there in shock. All along I'd thought everyone was pushing Norm into being the killer. Now it appeared they really had taken a pigeon and made it into a hawk.

Turning the ignition, I noticed a dark sedan pulling out from a rear parking lot. It was hard to tell, but I thought there was a Smalley's Chocolates sticker on the bumper. It brought to my mind the sedan that had picked up Jerry from Smalley's that first night of bingo. My curiosity and a hunch took over. I floored the gas pedal to get behind the car for a closer look.

With only two vehicles between the sedan and me, I

was catching up and hopeful I'd see who was driving the car. Failing that, I'd get near enough to jot down the plate number.

One car between us and we were coming to a red light. I slowed to a stop. Then I felt myself pitch forward and strain against my seatbelt. The driver behind me had hit my bumper and she was motioning me to move off to the side. I slammed my hand against my steering wheel. "Hell, crap, poop!" I pulled into a Giant Eagle grocery store parking lot and stepped out of my car, my knees still knocking. Shaking my head in dumb frustration, I watched the dark sedan and the car between it and mine pull away as I exchanged insurance information with the conscientious woman who'd dented my bumper and scratched the paint.

Muttering to myself all the way to *Cannoli's*, I arrived there only to be bombarded by my aunt's questions about my saxophone lessons. My answers were monosyllable. I didn't mean to be rude. It was just that I had too much on my mind wondering about the case against Norm.

***

The next morning, I found out, as did all the citizens of Cleveland and beyond, about Norm's situation. It was all over the news. A witness had just come forth and identified Norm as being the man who sat behind her at a live music venue called Bennie's, in Cleveland Heights, an eastern suburb of Cleveland. She swore he'd been there the approximate time of Desiree's, or Joanna's, murder.

A reporter, his brows knit, wondered aloud into the camera, why the police hadn't pursued Norm's alibi more effectively. Hence, Norm Rockwell, the man who just yesterday, was a villain, now was lauded as an innocent tried and convicted by city officials who needed a quick resolution to a crime wave.

I turned the sound up when the scene switched to the police chief as he took the podium. He then read a pre-written statement in which he defended their reasoning for making the arrest and confirmed the police's determination to finding the Red Bow Killer. He didn't take any questions.

What followed on the news didn't shed any new light on the situation. The fact did remain, though, that no new murders had occurred since Norm was taken into custody. What ran through my mind was Griselli's request to find enough evidence to put Norm away for life or find the real Red Bow Killer.

Grabbing my car keys and saying good-bye to Charlie, I left my apartment vowing to do just that.

My first stop would be the office to see if Griselli had returned my call. It made me nervous that he'd insisted on his money back yet wasn't available to find out when to get it. What was even more disturbing was Gino's unwillingness to return the fee. My boss could be lazy and full-of-himself, even sometimes bending rules, but I'd never thought of him as a thief. Maybe he was, and I'd just turned a blind eye to it. I shook my head to rid myself of those ruminations. I couldn't afford to add any other problems to my list. But, try as I might to keep it at bay, the thought kept returning.

By the time I'd reached my destination, my mood was dark enough to diminish any glow from the sun. There'd been no return calls from Griselli, and Gino hadn't yet made an appearance.

Rather than stew over everything going on, I'd decided to put any information, even slightly related to the Red Bow killings, together. A big undertaking, since there were enough characters to populate a classic Russian novel.

Convinced a cup of tea would help me think, I went into the kitchen, only to recall we were out of tea bags. I grumbled to nobody and shuffled back to my desk.

Someone jiggled the handle on the office door and walked in. It was Timothy, Eileen's brother. Dark circles surrounded his eyes, making him look like an exhausted raccoon, but he was clean-shaven and his clothing neat.

I put on my gentlest smile. "How are you, Timothy?"

His voice was soft, bereft of energy. "You heard that guy, Rockwell, was released?"

Although I wasn't feeling so confident, I pumped it into my voice. "Yes. It must be hard to think that the man who took Eileen's life is still out there, but it doesn't mean he won't be found."

Though he nodded, Timothy's expression said he'd just about given up hope.

I shifted gears a bit. "Gino isn't here yet. I'm not sure when he'll come in."

He shrugged. "Might as well give this to you as to Gino." He reached into his Cleveland Indians logo jacket pocket and pulled out a thick beige envelope. "Before this all happened, Eileen gave me a box of what she called ancient memories to keep for her. I figured it was stuff from when we were kids. Anyway, I didn't have the stomach to open it until this morning." He nodded toward the envelope. "That was in the box. Maybe it's nothing, but I wanted you guys to take a look at it."

Excitement made my fingers a bit clumsy. It took me a minute to extract a small black notebook. The first few pages contained some names and addresses of stores in Pittsburgh.

Most interesting, though, were her notations of dates, next to which she'd written dollar amounts. These ranged from $1,000 at the top of the list to $1,500 later on. The last entry was ten years ago.

My heart began pounding hard enough to shake the building. When I flipped through the rest of the book a faded red ribbon sailed to the floor.

I could feel Timothy's eyes on me. To buy time for my voice to return, I leaned over and retrieved the ribbon, setting it on my desk. With great difficulty, I organized my thoughts. Choosing the right words was next to impossible, so I started with the safest observation. "These amounts she wrote down. Her salary?"

"And that?" He pointed at the ribbon.

I cleared my throat. "Nothing unusual about a red ribbon. This one could've come from anything; a box of candy…" The look on his face told me he wasn't buying my explanation. Understandable, since I didn't either.

He switched back to the dates. "My sister didn't make the kind of money she listed here. I saw some of her old paystubs."

My feeble attempts at diplomacy failed. "You should take this to the police, Timothy. Let them sort it out."

He scoffed. "Yeah, they've done such a bang-up job with evidence so far."

I couldn't disagree with him, but wasn't so sure I liked the direction in which this conversation seemed to be heading.

There was a touch of hope in his voice. "You and Gino could figure out if what's in this book had anything to do with Eileen's murder." When I hesitated, he pulled out a ragged checkbook from the envelope and opened it. "These deposits match the notations in that notebook."

Timothy wasn't going to say it, so I did. "You think the money came from something illegal?" My breath caught. "Blackmail?"

Chapter Twenty-Three

His voice was barely a whisper. "Whatever it was, I think it got her killed. Even ten years later."

I swallowed hard. "All the more reason to take this to the cops."

He shook his head firmly. "Not a chance. *You* look at this." He thrust the checkbook at me. "Whatever my sister did, I don't want the cops dragging her name through the muck."

Footsteps sounded, stopping me from any further argument.

"Hello?" It was Betty, dressed up as if ready for a night on the town in her deep blue, off-the-shoulder dress and strappy spiked heels. Her eyes strayed to Timothy then back to me. "Sorry, didn't mean to interrupt."

Timothy grabbed Eileen's notebook from my hands and scooped up the ribbon while I gave Betty a weak smile. "Gino's not in, but I'm sure he'll be here—"

Betty held up her hand, causing her heavy charm bracelet to jangle. "That's okay. He told me if I beat him here to wait in his office." Her face suddenly contorted with anger. "Did you hear they had the wrong guy for Rose's murder? I never thought Norm killed her. Jeez, he played an accordion!"

Timothy grumbled, "Cops don't know what they're doing. Gino and Claire could do a better job finding the SOB."

Her chin dimpled and quivered. "No justice yet for my poor sister." She shook it off and turned toward Gino's office. Either because of her high heels or the tightness of her dress, her steps were so tiny I thought it might be nighttime before she reached the chair across from Gino's desk.

Once Betty disappeared into Gino's office, Timothy demanded my pledge not to take the notebook to the police.

"Okay. I'll keep it between you, Gino, and me. For now." I didn't elaborate because, in truth, I didn't know how long that would be. Any opportunity to decide what to do next was eliminated when Gino came through the door.

He looked to his right and left and over his shoulder as if afraid the CIA were following him. "Hi, Timothy. Claire, you seen Betty?" Even his voice was jerky.

"She's in your office, waiting for you."

He patted his jacket pocket and swallowed hard. "I'm going in there." Like an action hero, Gino threw open the door to his office and leaped inside to do...*whatever*.

I shrugged in response to Timothy's questioning look. I was as in the dark as he.

Not for long. Soon we heard Betty release a joyful squeal. Then, less than a minute after that, the door sprang open and Betty paraded to my desk, holding her left arm out in front of her, wrist bent downward.

I squinted against the glare. *That new diamond ring must weigh a ton.*

Gino followed Betty, an uncertain grin on his face. I couldn't tell if it was happiness and relief or plain old disbelief over what he'd done.

"We're engaged!" Betty jumped up and down as if

skipping a tiny rope.

Timothy recovered before me and stuck out his hand to Gino. "Congratulations."

I blinked hard to clear the shock from my mind. "Yeah. Congratulations. To both of you." The smile on my face was so tight, I worried my lips might snap.

Is that what he did with Griselli's retainer money? My only hope was that Gino had enough left over to pay his hospital bills when that 'loan' came due.

Gino was still grinning when he went to the kitchen and returned with a bottle of sparkling wine and some glasses. "We'll do a proper celebration later, but for now, let's drink to this happy occasion."

Timothy declined, "Been on the wagon too short a time to have just one glass."

After this morning's events, I welcomed the alcohol, saluting the happy couple. I downed the fizzy drink.

Betty set her empty glass on my desk. "Excuse me. Got to go to the little girl's room. All this excitement…"

As she was going out, another person was coming in.

My voice was high enough to crack my wine glass. "Mr. Griselli. I've been trying to reach you." If my suspicions were right about where Gino had gotten the ring money, maybe I could stall Griselli long enough for my boss to escape.

Griselli scowled. "I heard your messages. I'm also smart enough to know when I'm getting the runaround. Figured the best way to get my money back was to show up and surprise you guys."

Gino ran his finger around the inside of his collar. "Now what's this? You want a refund?" Gino's talent for feigning ignorance failed him.

"Francini, you knew damn well I wanted my money

back." The man clenched his teeth. "I need it now. No excuses." He reached inside the breast pocket of his coat and my breath caught. Instead of a gun, he pulled out a handkerchief and wiped his brow.

Gino released a shaky breath. He must have thought the same as me. "I'd be happy to return your money, but—"

I interrupted. "But we've already got a great lead on who the real killer is." If only Timothy would agree to share it.

Gino's eyebrows shot up and then quickly knit. "Yeah…We do?"

Timothy, bless his soul, stepped up. "Did the same guy who killed my sister kill someone you loved?"

Griselli stared at Timothy through hooded eyes. "One in the same. Eileen."

Timothy plopped down onto the closest chair, and Griselli went through his whole story, ending with his coming to Gino for help finding her killer.

After he listened to the entire story, Timothy scratched his chin. "But if you loved my sister, why do you want them to end their investigation?"

"That's not what I *want*. But I need the dough back." He gritted his teeth. "My ex-wife wants her alimony. Judge told me in no uncertain terms to give it to her." He paused. "Besides, I'm pretty good at deducing people's character, and I think this little lady here will dig until she uncovers the truth. Regardless of payment."

Gino waved Griselli's comment about me aside. "But you had a wad of cash when you came here."

"Let's put it this way. A man can incur debts pretty fast around here." Griselli's face darkened. "Now where's my money?"

Gino stood straight, planting his feet firmly. "I don't have it."

Griselli turned to me, but I could only shrug as if I had no clue what Gino had done with the money. Much as I wanted to yell at Gino for being an idiot, it was my duty to protect him. I could only hope Betty and her diamond wouldn't return until Griselli left.

Then it happened. Betty re-entered the office. No doubt wrapped in her own excitement, she was oblivious to any tension in the air. "Oops, guess I'm interrupting again." Giggling like a teenager, she gave Gino a peck. "I better be on my way anyway. There's a lot of planning to do. Now that Gino and me are engaged." She held her left hand in front of her face and wiggled her ring finger. "Gorgeous, ain't it?" Then, without waiting for an answer, she said goodbye.

I held my breath, hoping Griselli wouldn't figure out where his money had gone. But he wasn't an idiot. From the look on his face, I was afraid he would grab Betty and slice off her finger. But no, he allowed her to leave, fingers intact. Once she was gone, fists clenched, teeth bared, Grisselli asked, "That rock how you spent my dough?"

To my surprise, Gino stood his ground, wobbly though it was. "I'd already bought the ring before you asked for your money back. Don't worry, though. You'll get it. Tuesday, next week."

"You blew my money on a ring? If I was a younger man…" Griselli punched his fist into his other hand, no doubt wishing it'd been Gino's jaw. "Not only did you use my money dishonestly, but you're too ignorant to know you're playing a sucker's game, getting married. Sure, they're sweet in the beginning. Until the ring's on their finger. Then they figure it's as good as through your nose."

Gino shook his head, "Betty's not like that."

"No?" Despite his skeptic question, Griselli's face softened. "Maybe not. Eileen wasn't like that either." His eyes misted over. "She was real special."

Timothy spoke softly, "Yeah, my sister sure was. But somebody still killed her."

Griselli spun around as if he'd forgotten Eileen's brother was still there. "Tell me about her. What was she like before..."

Timothy's eyes matched Griselli's for moistness. "She was funny, generous, and real smart. Wish I'd spent more time with her." One eyebrow rose as he stared at Griselli. "How'd you know her?"

Griselli repeated what he'd told Gino and me earlier, about his relationship with Eileen.

Timothy's mouth dropped open. Then, "You're Joey G?"

"She told you about me?" Griselli's face lit up.

"In her letters. She thought the world of you." Timothy's eyebrows lowered. "You came to the wake, didn't you?"

"Yeah. Couldn't stay away."

The two men shook and then broke into a manly hug.

While I was relieved to see the lovefest, I was anxious to return to the notebook and Eileen's Pittsburgh activities. I asked Griselli if he could shed light on the subject.

"I can sure as hell try."

"Timothy?" If looks could persuade, I hoped mine would convince Timothy it was all right to share.

For a tense moment I thought he wouldn't agree to show his information. With a sigh, he slowly withdrew the notebook and turned to the entries we'd discussed earlier. He didn't mention the ribbon he'd dropped into his pocket.

Griselli squinted and his mouth twisted from side to side as he studied each line.

I held my breath, hoping he'd be able to lead us past the dead ends we kept running into.

Still peering at the entries, Griselli pointed to what appeared to me like a squiggly ink leak. "Look at this. There's two m's there. My guess is it stands for Music Man."

Timothy rubbed the knuckles of his one hand with the other. "You think she took money from a guy she never even mentioned to me? Why the hell would she do that?"

Gino patted Timothy's shoulder. "Take it easy, buddy. We'll get some answers."

Not wanting to guess at those answers, I lowered my face into the notebook. Sure enough, although sometimes it was faded beyond casual notice, that same squiggle showed up after each dollar amount. "Timothy, did Eileen have a date book or calendar for that time?"

"I don't think so." Timothy's voice oozed disappointment.

"What about the ribbon?" I couldn't leave that out.

"What ribbon?" Gino looked squarely at his friend, who reluctantly removed it from his pocket. Gino stepped back as if confronted by a rattlesnake. "That what I think it is?"

Waving Gino's question aside, I asked, "We don't know. Mr. Griselli, any ideas?"

He shrugged. "Could be from anything…"

I returned to the notebook, wondering aloud, "Was each notation made the same day of the week? Like on a Friday?"

Using my computer, I pulled up each date noted and ascertained all were Mondays.

I asked Griselli, "Any ideas as to what days she saw Music Man?"

"Weekends the guy had a regular gig at the Sunset Club. She told me that Sunday nights, they'd go out until all hours. At least what passed for all night on Sunday in Pittsburgh."

His eyes got a far-away look to them. "Until one day she just disappeared. I got a quick phone message from her saying goodbye." He snapped back to the here-and-now. "That was it."

His phone buzzed and he pulled it out. Scowling, he said, "Gotta go. If anybody asks, you never saw me." He took a menacing step toward Gino. "I'll be here Tuesday morning at nine to pick up my money. If you don't have it, I'll find your girlfriend and rip that ring right off her finger. *Cabishe*?"

Gino gave him a curt nod.

Griselli, with one more evil-eye glance toward Gino, departed.

Silent, I sank deeper into my chair. Timothy looked as if he'd just learned the Tooth Fairy stole money instead of leaving it.

Gino, whose mouth never met a question too delicate to voice, asked, "So, do you both think Eileen was involved with the murders of all those women?"

I could almost hear Timothy's teeth grinding. Before he could say anything, I jumped in. "That ribbon could be from anything and the entries—"

Timothy's hand went up. "Save it, Claire. I appreciate you trying to spare my feelings, but…"

Gino, at last grasping at diplomacy, interrupted. "Dumb, my even asking. Of course, she wasn't. We'll get to the bottom of this. Hey Timothy, why don't you and me get some coffee? We can figure out what to do next."

"Only if you and Claire promise not to take Eileen's stuff to the cops."

"We swear it. Right, Claire?"

I bit my lower lip and nodded, mentally crossing my fingers behind my back. "Before you go, Timothy, do you have access to Eileen's most current bank statement?"

"I already checked it. My name was on it too. It only had $1,000."

"If that's all settled, Timothy, go on ahead and I'll meet you at Blackbirds." Gino turned to me and whispered, "See if we have any invoices due."

Once both men were gone I sat at my computer, shaking my head. Gino needed money or Griselli would likely take it from his hide. Timothy had evidence linked to the Red Bow Killer. I had to decide which I'd work on. Rationalization came to my rescue. Gino got himself into the tar pit. The women who'd been killed hadn't done anything wrong except for maybe playing bingo. I blew out a breath, hoping to release some residual guilt for not helping Gino right away.

First thing to do was to see if I could find out Music Man's real name. I looked up the Sunset Club for a phone number. It was a long shot, but a girl had to start somewhere.

Somewhere turned out to be nowhere. The club was still in existence, but the new owners couldn't provide me with any information. I rested my chin in my hands, thinking about my next move. Inspiration came in the form of a notation in the back of Eileen's notebook. It read, "Lori," with a phone number next to it.

No telling who Lori was or what she knew, but those answers could be just a phone call away.

The phone rang several times. Either Lori no longer was at this number or, just as likely, wasn't about to answer a call from an unfamiliar number. But then I heard a click and, "Thanks for calling Hairtastic. This is Lori."

I talked fast, afraid she'd hang up on me. "Lori, my name is Claire DeNardo. I'm a private investigator working for the brother of Eileen O'Donnell."

Her response was a cautious, "Oka-a-y."

"We found your name and number in Eileen's notebook. I was wondering if you could answer a couple questions."

"Are you working with the cops? Is she in trouble?"

While being murdered was awful, I could truthfully say Eileen wasn't in trouble. Since Lori seemed unaware of Eileen's death, I answered with a brief, "No, she isn't. And no, I'm not working with the cops. As I said, I'm working on behalf of her brother, Timothy. Sounds like you remember her."

Lori's voice remained guarded. "Yeah, I did her hair and we got to be good friends."

"Did you know the guy she was dating? A musician?"

"Never met him, but Eileen talked about him. Music Man."

Hopes up, I asked, "Did she ever tell you his real name?"

After a moment that seemed to last forever, she asked, "What's this about?"

"I'm sorry, but Eileen has passed away and we're trying to contact him."

"No! Oh! Poor Eileen. I really liked her. She was great." Her voice choked and I waited a moment for her to recover.

Then I coaxed, "Her boyfriend's name?"

She sniffled, "Oh, yeah. I thought she dumped him before she left town. Anyway, I'm not sure what his last name was, but his first was the name of a tree."

"Maple? Palm?" When she didn't respond, "Elm?"

"No. None of those." She released a breath into the phone. "Now I remember. It was Birch."

"Are you sure that wasn't his last name?"

"Nope." She sounded surer now. "It was Birch. I remember because it was so weird I thought he made it up."

"Is there anything else you remember?"

"Sorry. It was a long time ago. Never met Eileen's brother, but would you give him my condolences? Tell him she was a good person."

A soft whoop slipped from my lips the minute I hung up with Lori. This was the first clue and it was a good one. After all, how many men who lived in Pittsburgh ten years ago could be named Birch?

It turned out he was more elusive than I thought. It was quitting time and I was no further in the investigation. On top of that, I hadn't done any reconnaissance to find unpaid invoices as Gino had asked.

I needed to leave for my second job at *Cannoli's*, but I had begun to worry. Gino hadn't returned to the office and wasn't answering my texts. All I could do at that point was hope Griselli hadn't changed his mind about waiting until Tuesday. I said a quick prayer Gino was all right and promised myself I'd carefully pick through all the invoices first thing in the morning.

Just as I was locking up the office, Gino appeared. He looked even more disheveled than usual, with his shirt halfway in and halfway out of his trousers. He had a stain on his collar and his tie was askew.

"Are you okay, Gino?"

"Sure. I'm okay. As okay as a guy with a new fiancé and a price on his head can be." He slumped against the wall, his usually coiffed dark brown hair, probably dyed, flopping onto his forehead. "Gotta get that money somehow." The slurring of his words told me he'd been imbibing, no doubt hoping to find the solution in alcohol. A fool's game at best.

I told myself not to feel sorry for him. You reap what you sow. He brought it on himself, etc. But my Catholic upbringing also told me to be kind toward another, even if the other is sometimes a jerk. Besides, I cared about the guy and it scratched at my heart to see him like this.

I patted his shoulder, "We'll find a way. I know it."

He placed his hand over mine. "You're a great kid, Claire. Yeah, we will." He gave me a brave smile. "Now, you better go or you'll be late to Lena's."

By the time I reached the staircase, Gino had disappeared into his office.

***

Cannoli's was busy, so my aunt barely had time to greet me. I slipped an apron on and went behind the counter. Business didn't slow until close to closing time. That's when Ed sauntered in, still wearing his security guard duds.

Aunt Lena's face lit up when she saw him, and she cooed, "I'm a sucker for a man in a uniform."

Ed grinned like a teenage boy with a gift card to a gaming store. "She's beautiful. *And* she can bake." He made his way to her and they kissed briefly. He then greeted me with, "What's up, kiddo?"

"As a matter of fact, quite a bit. Aunt Lena, mind if I take a break to fill Ed in on an assignment. That's if he wants it."

My aunt pursed her lips. "Okay, but not too long. We've got a lot to do if we want to get out of here at a decent hour. And, Claire, it better not be something dangerous. I want him around a long time."

Ed and I adjourned to the kitchen, where I explained the situation with Eileen's notebook and Griselli's information. I left out the bit about Gino owing Griselli. That was Gino's story to tell, if he so chose.

"Do you think you could do some digging to find this Birch guy?"

Ed rubbed his chin. "Suppose I could ask around. I know some guys from Pittsburgh. One's a drummer. You can never tell."

As was always the case, I was grateful to know Ed. We'd gotten off to a bad start when we first met. I almost ran him over. It was while I was investigating a murder at his workplace. But since then, he'd been a godsend to me.

Chapter Twenty-Four

Exhausted, I fell asleep right away that night. Not exactly a restful sleep though, since I dreamt that Gino was being pursued by a creature with diamonds for eyes but who otherwise resembled Griselli. Making the dream even more unsettling, I was unable or unwilling to help Gino.

When I awakened, Charlie's head was resting on my pillow, his doggy breath warm on my face. I'd finally given in to his cries last night and allowed him in bed.

As soon as I sat up, he seemed to come to life. Even though I was still drowsy, I put the leash on him and we stepped outside. He was getting bigger and harder to manage by the day. If I didn't enroll him in obedience school, he'd soon be out of control.

We'd just returned from our walk-and-tug when my phone rang. It was Corrigan.

His voice was brittle. "Turn on Channel Five."

My belly tightened. This could not be good.

Indeed, it wasn't. A reporter was talking into the camera, "...There's been another murder involving a red ribbon, in Lakewood. The victim's name has not been released pending family notification."

I muted the television, my heart heavy enough to sink the Queen Mary. "Brian, I'm so sorry. Do you have any suspects?"

He barked a humorless laugh, "You mean besides Rockwell? Who, incidentally, has made himself scarce? But we're looking for him. We found the woman about a mile from Corey's Bingo, behind a Giant Eagle Store. Same M.O. as all the others."

"Sounds like you're planning on doing a version of 'rounding up the usual suspects.'" I immediately wanted to un-say those words. *This is no way to support him.*

"Unless we get a break in this case, we don't have any other leads." He sounded defensive, and I couldn't blame him. "And the killings didn't start again until Rockwell was released."

My focus needed to be on helping him catch this killer. I believed that's what Corrigan wanted too but was reluctant to admit it. After all, with previous murder cases he'd made it a point to keep me on a need-to-know basis, and to him I had no need to know anything.

It didn't take a genius to figure out the enormous pressure he was facing, with the Captain, the public, and his own conscience. I went into 'fix-it' gear and weighed my options.

On one hand I'd told Griselli I wouldn't bring his name into anything. Also on that hand was my promise to Timothy not to reveal his information to the cops. The other hand represented all the women who'd died. If I had a third hand, it'd stand for the fact that the man I loved was sinking. His career and his self-confidence were at stake.

Clearing my throat so the reluctant words would come out, I said, "We need to talk."

After getting off the phone with Corrigan, I left a quick message on the office phone, telling Gino I'd be late to work. What I didn't tell him was that I was meeting with Corrigan for a cup of tea and confessions.

When the man in my life showed up at The Coffee Cup, surprise must have been evident on my face. To be blunt, he looked like something the cat had played with, attempted to eat, and then spit out. Dark circles couldn't hide the deepened lines around his eyes. I wanted to wrap him in a blanket and give him hot cocoa. He needed a haircut and was working on a five o'clock shadow at nine thirty in the morning.

"Yeah, I know. I look like hell. But seeing you is heaven." His dimples were as irresistible as ever. "You said we needed to talk. This isn't *the* talk, is it?"

"What? No. God, no!" Suddenly I was wondering what he'd say if I did ask him where this relationship was heading. With a quick blink of my eyes, I took my brain off that road. At least for now. For now, there were women's lives to save.

"This is about the Red Bow Killer." I raised my hand, palm facing him. "Let me get all the way through what I have to say. No interruptions, okay?"

The look of relief on his face when he learned this wasn't a conversation about our relationship was quickly replaced with knit brows and a frown. With a deep sigh, he said, "Okay. Now what is it?"

The words didn't exactly spill from my mouth. Dancing around Griselli's name wasn't easy. Somehow I managed. Skirting around the notebook was even more of a challenge. I finally settled with telling him about my conversation with Eileen's hairdresser, Lori, ending with my unsuccessful search for the guy named Birch.

True to his pledge, Corrigan listened without saying a

word. When I finished, he took a sip of his coffee and after carefully setting down his cup, asked, "What aren't you telling me, Claire? What does this tree guy have to do with all these murders?" His voice was even, but his hand was gripping his cup so tightly it was a wonder he didn't crush it.

While I knew finding the killer should have a higher priority than keeping Eileen's notebook a secret, I still balked at betraying Timothy's confidence. "My sources..."

He laid his forearms on the table and leaned towards me. "You're tying my hands, Claire. Who are your sources? What do they have? If you're going to help me, then, dammit, help me." The vein in his temple, the one I think of as his aggravation vein, gyrated.

I bit my lower lip and debated with myself. One toe in the water wasn't enough. To be of any assistance, I had to get soaked. "Okay, I'll tell you all about it. Give me until four this afternoon." Somehow I'd have to convince Timothy that turning over the evidence to Corrigan was the best route to take. My churning gut told me that wouldn't be an easy task.

Right now, though, I had to seize this opportunity to get answers to my own questions. "What can you tell me about this latest murder?"

He hesitated, pressing his lips together tightly for a moment. "All right. I'm trusting you, Claire. Don't let me down." He pulled out his notepad. "The victim's name is, or was, Rebecca Singer. Forty-three. Single. Lived alone. She'd last been seen alive playing bingo at Corey's Bingo Center. No witnesses to the crime." He closed his pad. "That's all we have so far."

My brain was whirling so fast, it should have made me dizzy. Another murder tied to bingo. What was it about that game that spurred the killer to do what he did?

Corrigan rubbed his face and the full extent of his exhaustion shown through again. "Every turn I've taken with this has led to a dead end and another corpse. I've got to get this guy." His shoulders slumped as if the weight of all the victims' bodies had been dropped on him.

I tilted my head in a question. "So you're asking, in your roundabout way, for my help? I mean, besides what we just talked about."

His eyes scanned the room, as if he was afraid of being caught talking with me. "Yeah. I guess I am. Not, I repeat, not to have you track down the killer yourself. My feelings on that haven't changed. I don't want you hurt. No more going to bingo parlors. Please."

I was flattered that, after pushing me to the outside on so many cases, he would actually welcome my help. But I couldn't just drop my own pursuit of the man who'd snuffed out so many lives, especially that of my beloved babysitter, Vincenza Amato. I had to get this guy for her. On top of all that, it'd taken me numerous murder cases to gain what small amount of confidence I had in my abilities. Would what was essentially working for Corrigan end up with me losing my independence?

I realized while I'd been staring at my hands lost in these thoughts, Corrigan had been watching me, no doubt calculating my response. When I raised my head, it hit me how much he needed my consent. I sighed, understanding that I couldn't agree to stop my own investigation, but I could be more cooperative. "What exactly do you want?"

He grabbed my hands. "You let me know immediately whenever you get any new information or even a suspicion of something going on. That's all I ask. And that you stay away from any hint of danger." He smirked. "I don't want to have to rescue you."

I yanked my hands from his. "Don't worry. You won't have to save me from any villain who's tying me to the railroad tracks. I can take care of myself."

He harrumphed, but gave no retort. Maybe he was just too tired.

Draining my cup, I said, "I better go. I have people to talk with and information to dig up."

He rose from his chair. "Me too. But I expect to hear from you in six hours or less. That would be by four this afternoon."

"I can tell time and even add or subtract. Talk to you then." My display of confidence was a sham. Timothy had been adamant about not sharing Eileen's information with the police. The thought of breaking my promise to him made me feel like a weasel. Surely there was a way to convince him to share. There just had to be.

***

Luck is something I rarely encounter. But it shone its sunny face on me that morning. Timothy not only answered his phone but even agreed to meet and talk.

The girl behind the counter at The Coffee Cup gave me a knowing smile when I showed up for the second time that morning with a different man. Thank God, Timothy, with his obvious comb-over and belly that lapped over his belt, didn't notice.

He and I found a table in the back of the cafe and sat across from each other. Before I could say a word, he began tapping his fingers against his cup. "You want to take Eileen's notebook to the cops." His jaw was set and his eyes held a challenge.

To convince him that surrendering the notebook to the police was best, I bent the truth a bit. Okay, I twisted it like a strongman curves an iron rod. "The police have just hired me as a consultant on the Red Bow murders. So it wouldn't be as if I just turned over Eileen's notebook and walked away. I'll have some control over how it's interpreted." My words fell over each other, repeating how vital his evidence was, not only in solving Eileen's murder, but possibly even the Pittsburgh killings. I even appealed to his conscience, pointing out the possibility of other women dying if his information didn't come to light.

He hung his head in silence.

I went on to tell him what my call to Lori had revealed.

Still, he didn't lift his head, nor say a word.

I softened my voice. "Timothy?"

He finally looked me in the eye. "I'm counting on you to use the notebook wisely."

I blew out a breath. "To the best of my ability."

With a curt nod of his head, he broke eye contact. "I won't give you the ribbon back. If you turn it over to the cops, God knows how they'll interpret it and Eileen can't defend herself now."

There'd be no argument from me about the ribbon. I was relieved he at least had enough confidence in me to let me turn over the notebook. "Understandable. But if you change your mind..."

"I won't." With that, he stood. "I gotta get outta here." He walked out leaving me feeling like Judas.

I stared at the exit for a moment, half expecting him to return and demand the notebook back. It wouldn't have surprised me if he had. With the evidence now completely in my control, the fluttering in my stomach intensified.

I got into my car and drove to the office, obeying all the speed limits. At every stop, I allowed other drivers to pull in front of me. But none of that made me feel any better of a person. Just a better driver. Even understanding Eileen's notebook could be of value in finding her killer didn't help. The belief I was a turncoat stuck to me like gum to the bottom of a shoe.

Once I laid my purse on my desk, I was determined to heave my guilt into the waste can. It was getting in the way of my current task, finding invoices for Gino. I shuddered to imagine how Griselli might rearrange my boss's face if he didn't get his money back.

I shuffled through a huge paper file, grousing not for the first time, over why Gino insisted on hard copies instead of a computer spreadsheet.

About a third of the way through, an invoice stopped me cold. It was a duplicate of an old bill we'd recently collected on. Back then, the name on that invoice had been meaningless to me. Now I clutched the paper so tightly the top of it ripped.

Wolden. Jerry Wolden. The name smacked my brain so hard my head whipped back. The elderly man from bingo. Why did he keep popping up—at bingo, the library, Eileen's workplace? And now he could be the uncle of a murderous nephew? I tried to recall what else Gino had told me about the case. Either the memory hadn't stuck or was buried under a ton of other information. I pounded my temples with both my hands, trying to shake the memory loose.

Praying Gino's filing ability prior to my re-employment was better than his punctuality I hurried over to the file cabinets.

Fifteen minutes later, I located the handwritten notes on Wolden. Skimming through them, I recalled the gist of his concern. He had suspected his nephew, who now lived with him, of killing his own mother, Ann. Ann had been Wolden's sister.

I stood in front of the open cabinet drawer and flipped through the report, my eyes darting across the pages, searching for the nephew's name and other details about him. The information wasn't included. Not anywhere. That's when I realized page three of the report was missing. I slammed the file drawer hard. *Damn, damn, double damn!*

Taking a deep breath, I reopened the cabinet drawer. The missing page had probably been filed in the wrong folder. My heart sank to my knees when I thought how long it might take to find it.

The office phone rang. It was Ed.

"Hey, kiddo. Just talked with the drummer I knew from Pittsburgh. He recalled a guy, a guitar player, with a weird name. Thinks it could've been Birch. Says the guy used to play with a group called the Wild Ones. My buddy also said he thinks he has a promo picture of the Wild Ones, with the guy you're looking for." He took a breath. "Anyway, I gave him your number and he says when he finds the picture, he'll fax it to you."

"That's wonderful, Ed. In the meantime, was he able to remember what the guy looked like?"

"I asked, but he said it was too long ago to recall. Sorry."

"Yeah, not surprising. Great job, though, Ed. I'll look at what he sends and then take it to Corrigan."

I told him about working with Corrigan, Ed was sympathetic.

"The guy needs a break before this case breaks him. Hope this arrangement pans out for him. And for you."

Probably looking for some sympathy for myself, I recounted my experience with the lost page to Ed.

"Did you check Gino's desk?"

"Why would it be there?"

"Why would it be missing from the report?"

"You've got a point." I was anxious to return to my search. "Thanks for your help, Ed."

Off the phone, I wondered if Ed could be right. It was unlikely, but maybe he was. I'd look there later, after the file cabinets.

Mentally I replaced having a good night with having a long night, because that's what it would be.

I didn't get very far when my phone rang again.

It was Suzy. I moaned. With all that'd been going on lately, I'd forgotten about my duty as maid-of-honor.

"Claire, I'm so sorry to bother you at work, but if you're free this Saturday morning, would you be willing to look at wedding dresses with me? Maybe you could also find a bridesmaid's dress."

Her voice sounded so sweet it made the heat from my guilt burn even hotter. "Of course, Suzy. And I'm so sorry for not calling you sooner. It's just…" Any excuse would sound so insignificant. This was my future stepmom I'd been ignoring.

"Don't worry about it, Claire. You're a busy woman. And it's just as easy for me to pick up the phone. So how about we grab breakfast at Second Watch at Crocker Park and then start shopping? Around nine? I'm bound to find something with all those stores there."

"Something traditional, like a white dress?"

She laughed, "That boat sailed before you were even born. No, I want something that'll reflect who I am."

A tight-fitting dress with rhinestones. I quickly banished that uncharitable vision. "Sounds good. I'll just let my aunt know I need the day off."

"Umm. You don't have to do that. I already squared it with her."

Suzy was getting the hang of handling this family. "Great, see you tomorrow morning."

The crammed-together folders were still waiting for me, and I returned to searching for the missing page three when my phone rang yet again. Frustrated at the multiple interruptions, I was about it let it go into voicemail. Then I saw it was Gino.

"Hey, Claire. I, uh, won't be in the office today. Or tomorrow. I'm working on a deal."

"To pay back Griselli?" I rubbed my forehead, feeling a headache coming on.

"Yeah. Do me a favor, though." That approaching headache galloped across my scalp. "If Betty shows up, asking where I am, play dumb. Okay?"

I didn't have to play. Allowing myself to get involved with any plan or deal with Gino *was* dumb. "But I don't—"

"Thanks, you're a doll." He was gone.

Enough. So many needs, wants and other people's interests were hitting me, I felt as if I were sitting on one of those carnival dunk-'em seats. Just a matter of time before somebody hit the bull's eye and I dropped into the water tank.

I was left alone again, but didn't have the patience to look for what amounted to scrounging through a cyclone of papers. To my relief, the photo Ed's friend had promised finally came in. It was blurry, so I grabbed the magnifying glass Gino kept in his top drawer. I peered at the photo again. The man Ed's friend had thoughtfully noted as Birch was tying a big bow around some smiling groupie's neck. Looked like laughs all around, but I wondered if the bow was red.

A glance at the clock reminded me of my promise to

Corrigan. I grabbed my purse and keys, hoping I could make it to the police station by four.

I arrived with two minutes to spare. Corrigan was waiting outside the station for me. He hustled me into an interrogation room. "Never know who's listening. What have you got for me?"

I handed him Eileen's notebook and told him all I knew, even about the ribbon that escaped from the notebook's pages. I concluded, "Eileen must have had something on this Birch guy. Something bad enough that he kept looking for her, even ten years later."

He rose from his chair. "And you think this is something concerning the women who died in Pittsburgh *and* the murders here?"

"Don't forget. Eileen was the first victim in Cleveland. That's not a coincidence."

"Ten years after the Pittsburgh killings? Come on, the murders might be related, or maybe someone's a copycat, but..."

I waved the fax. "And look at this. This one's Birch."

His brows drew together. "Girl's wearing a bow around her neck. But lots of people used bows. And she doesn't look like she minds." He caught my look of determination. "Okay, okay, we'll contact the authorities in Pittsburgh. See if we can get a lead on this Birch guy."

My mouth formed the words to tell him about Gino's investigation for Jerry Wolden, but I stopped myself. He would just think I was wasting his time.

Chapter Twenty-Five

Frustrated at my inability to move forward on the case, I left work to take Charlie out, then arrived at *Cannoli's* just in time for my second job. Thankfully, we were busy, but no new drama presented itself. As the evening wore on, my energy level slowly dove to near zero. I had a cup of black coffee toward the end of my shift, hoping it would get me through my nighttime search of Gino's desk for the missing report page.

***

Yawning, I unlocked the office door, turned on all the lights, and locked the door behind me. *Can't be too safe.*

I stepped into Gino's office and realized, with dismay, his desk was piled high with papers turned every which way, some smoothed, some crumpled. None in any order. I scooped up one stack and leafed through them. Nothing I needed. Same with the next stack.

Fatigue was getting the upper hand on me. I plopped into a chair with stack number three and began sifting through the papers. I didn't get far when I heard a noise. Removing my gun from my near-by purse, I aimed it at the door.

"Claire?" It was Gino, looking even more disheveled than when I'd seen him the previous day. Despite the unseasonable chill in the mid-June air, he'd replaced his usual sports jacket for a polyester shirt that looked as if it'd been left over from disco night. "What're you doing here?"

"I think we might have a break in the Red Bow killings."

His heavy-lidded eyes opened wide. "What is it?"

After giving him a quick rundown of what had occurred today, I added, "If my guess is right, the nephew whose name is on page three of the report you completed for Jerry Wolden is our killer. But that page is missing."

"Can't be." He rubbed the heavy stubble on his chin. But if it is, we've gotta find it." He glanced at his watch. "But not now. I got somebody coming here to talk business. Time for you to go home."

He practically shoved me out the door and on my way down the stairs, I saw why. A heavyset, olive-skinned man in an expensive suit was heaving himself up the stairs. I could smell his expensive cologne as he passed by. Why he was there was unclear to me, but I was sure it wasn't to hire Gino to track down his Bible. Even as I pulled out of the office parking lot, a part of me wanted to go back inside and save Gino from whatever his scheme was.

But my boss was a grown-up and would have to deal with his actions. Not that I really bought that, but Charlie needed to go outside and, unlike Gino, he hadn't made his bed.

Good thing I'd made that choice because as soon as I opened his cage door, my poor pup ran to the door, whimpering. I was so anxious to get him outdoors I pulled my gun from my purse and paused only long enough to lock my door behind me.

Charlie tugged and pulled at his leash to catch up with two couples who looked like they were trying to get their 10,000 steps in before the end of the day. We followed them as they did a loop past my apartment building. Feeling safe, I finally managed to yank Charlie away and we turned into my building.

I sped up the stairs, hoping to tire Charlie out even more. Once we reached my floor, we jogged to my apartment door. It was ajar.

Chapter Twenty-Six

Charlie let out a low growl and the hairs on my arms stood up. I pulled my gun from my waistband. Not wanting Charlie to get hurt, I wrapped his leash handle around the doorknob so he couldn't run in. On legs that felt as sturdy as paper clips, I took a step inside. Far enough to reach my phone. I was ready to call 911 when Charlie freed his leash and dashed into my apartment, barking as if to chase out the demons. I followed him.

Nobody was in the living room or the kitchen. Fear clawed deeper into my heart as I entered the bedroom and bathroom. The apartment was empty and seemed to be the same as when I left it.

I was ungluing my hand from my gun when my insides turned to slush. I'd been in such a hurry to take Charlie outside I'd dropped my purse on the floor. But now it sat on the table. Someone had broken into my apartment and moved it. What had they taken? I grabbed the purse and dumped the contents on the sofa, tearing through everything. My wallet still contained one dollar and 59 cents and my driver's license, tissues, mirror; nothing was missing.

Should I call the police or not? And say what? Somebody picked my purse off the floor? Waiting for my breathing to go back to normal, I decided not to report the break-in. The calmer I got, the less I wanted Corrigan to get wind of what happened and tie it back to my involvement on this case. I didn't need him on my back just now.

***

That night, Charlie, growing bigger by the day, lay curled up beside me on the sofa. Needless to say, I didn't get much sleep. Even with my dog and my gun next to me.

Feeling foggy-brained the next morning, I dragged myself off the sofa and into the shower to prepare for work. The queasy feeling about someone being in my apartment stuck with me. *Would they return?* The thought of Charlie being an easy target rubbed my conscience the wrong way. So rather than putting him back into his cage, I left him to roam around my place freely. After murmuring to him to be a good boy, I double-checked to make sure I'd locked up my apartment tight.

When I arrived at the office, the door was ajar and Gino was slumped over his desk. My heart jumped into my throat. Had Gino's plan with the thuggish-looking man gone awry? I rushed over, only to see he was just asleep.

Once my heart returned to its normal position, I nudged him. "Gino, wake up."

Eyelids fluttering, he finally sat up and stretched. He yawned, "Just resting."

"Are you all right?" Despite my intellectualizing that his problems were self-induced and not really my concern, I was worried about him. "That guy that came here last night…"

"Lou? I'm just doing him a favor, for which he'll pay pretty good."

A vision of Gino going to prison floated through my head. "Legal or not?"

He tipped his hand back and forth. "*Menzamenz.*"

"How could something be half-legal and half-not?"

Through gritted teeth, he said, "Look, I gotta pay Griselli back. I'll be damned if I let him take the ring from Betty."

I knew when to back off. And I wasn't his mother or his conscience. "Okay. But let's see if we can find out the name of Jerry Wolden's nephew." My eyebrows shot up. "You don't happen to remember if his name was Birch, do you?"

"Nah. I'd remember a weirdo name like that."

My phone rang and to my surprise, it was Todd Shotswell, asking about my appointment. "Claire, I know this is short notice, but I've had two cancellations for tomorrow and was wondering if you'd be interested in moving your lesson up."

I wrinkled my nose. Humiliating myself again wasn't high on my priority at that moment. "Sorry, but I have plans for that morning."

"Actually, I was thinking about the late afternoon, say three? If after this time, you're convinced the sax in your hands is an instrument of torture, I'll refund all your money."

"You're that confident I'll be better?"

"Yes, I am."

I could've just told him I wasn't interested anymore, especially if he was interested in me in a romantic way. But the thought of getting all my money back was too tempting, especially knowing I had a bridesmaid's dress to buy. "Sure. All right." My only reservation now was where the money for this second lesson was coming from since it was no longer part of a case.

I got off the call but didn't have a lot of time to ponder that question because Gino let out a loud whoop and dashed toward me waving a paper. "Found it! Found that sucker!"

"Page three? Let me see!" I snatched it from his hand and

skimmed through the note. My shoulders dropped in disappointment. It wasn't page three of the Wolden report. It was a letter some guy had written to Gino saying he owed Gino $500.

I sank into my desk chair. Great news for Gino, assuming he could collect, but not for my Red Bow Killer investigation.

Gino, no doubt noticing my disappointment claimed, "Well it's good news for me. Now I'll just need $3,500 more for Griselli. And that's what Lou will pay me for finding—somebody." He looked past me to the door. "Better go home, change clothes and collect on this." He hit the paper with the back of his hand. "I'll see you as soon as I can."

My boss hadn't been gone more than ten minutes when Lou, Gino's mysterious client, walked into the office. He was wide enough to block any light between him and the doorway. "Hey, you Gino's secretary?"

His voice rang out, but I didn't even see his lips move under his heavy mustache. "Sometimes. Can I help you? Or would you rather speak with Gino?" I hoped for the latter.

"Nah, you'll do fine. Tell him we located the person he was supposed to find." He flipped through a wad of money and peeled off three hundred dollar bills. "Tell Gino this is for his trouble."

Without another word, the large man left without looking back, even as I shouted, "Don't you want a receipt?"

I peered down at the money in my hand. Not anywhere near what Gino had counted on. Thinking he didn't have any time to lose in collecting what he owed Griselli, I called him, but it immediately went into voicemail. Not wanting to leave him a message he'd lost out on his deal, I asked Gino to call me right away.

As I was deciding what to do next, Corrigan sauntered

into my office. He looked as disheveled as the previous day, but this time, there was a spark in his eyes. "Brian, what are you doing here?"

"Aren't you going to ask me to sit down?" His voice held a tiny bit of the old cockiness. A tingle went through me. *They'd caught the Red Bow Killer.*

"Are you alone?"

After I nodded, he continued. "The killer struck again last night. But he got sloppy. The victim survived."

I sucked in a breath. "She can identify him?"

His jaw worked hard as he considered his words. "She's unconscious. But the doctor's hopeful she'll come out of it. She's under heavy guard and almost nobody knows she's alive. It's gotta stay that way. If it gets out I told you, it could be my job."

"Why *did* you tell me?"

"Fair's fair. I asked you to inform me on everything you knew or found out. In return, I'd do the same, as long as it didn't put you in any danger."

My feelings were about as layered as lasagna. First, I was flattered and thrilled he'd confided in me, maybe even needed to. Second, I worried what would happen if the news did get out, and third, I was afraid the woman would die and the nightmare would continue. Topping all this was my concern over disappointing him and not living up to his expectations. Plus, that ever-present fear I'd lose my independence as a PI.

I never got to voice any of my concerns, though, because he got a call he had to take. A minute later, he hurried off. It was just as well. The last thing my favorite detective needed on his broad shoulders was an indecisive partner.

***

Alone once again, I continued to hunt for the missing page

until I was ready to scream from frustration. At four, I knew I had to leave for *Cannoli's.* There'd be no issues there, just pastries, family, and me. In between customers, I could plot my next steps if page three didn't show up. Such as calling Jerry Wolden myself.

But I should've known I wouldn't have the time. *Cannoli's* was mobbed when I got there and we just kept moving, loading cakes, brownies, cannoli's, and cookies onto the quickly emptying shelves. It wasn't until nine forty-five that we could sit and rest. That's when it started.

My aunt looked sideways at me. That meant she was plotting. "So I hear you're going with Suzy to look at bridal gowns."

Here it comes. "Not exactly bridal gowns. Just a dress for her to wear at her wedding."

She shrugged. "Same thing. Who else is going?"

"Nobody, as far as I know. Why?" I was on my guard.

"Seems to me, Suzy needs the perspective of a more mature woman in choosing her dress. People remember what the bride wore."

Yes, and who could forget my aunt's own recently worn wedding dress with the huge rose that looked as if it would devour her ample breasts and then go for the rest of her?

I threw my hands in the air. "If Suzy's okay with you coming to shop with her, who am I to object?"

Aunt Lena gave me a sharp nod, as if to show me the matter was settled. She'd tag along.

***

As soon as I opened my apartment door, there was Charlie, wiggling his hind end. He'd gotten into the magazines on the table. They were everywhere, but at least he hadn't ripped them apart. *Maybe he'd read them and could give me fashion tips.*

Not long after an uneventful walk with my pup was ended, my bed called. It also must have called to Charlie, since he climbed in with me. The next thing I knew, it was Saturday morning.

I dragged myself from my cozy bed, dreading the day. If the wedding dress hunt only involved Suzy and me, it would have been fun. With Aunt Lena along, it would most likely range from being a mere struggle to an outright battle.

Driving to Crocker Park, I daydreamed my aunt changed her mind and allowed Suzy to choose her own dress. *Pfff!* That was about as likely as Aunt Lena wearing a miniskirt and thigh-high boots to Mass.

I arrived at Second Watch at Crocker Park a few minutes before nine. Taking a deep breath and rolling my shoulders back, I entered the restaurant. Suzy was alone. For a brief moment, hope flowered in my chest, only to be plucked at the root when Aunt Lena dragged herself in. She used her hand to fan herself. “Whew. I had to park on the other side of this place. It’s this heat. It must be 90 degrees out there.” It was actually 74 degrees.

“Lena! How nice to see you!” Suzy’s smile didn’t entirely mask her surprise at my aunt’s appearance.

“I hope you’re okay with me tagging along. I’ve known Frank a long time and I figured I could help you pick out a dress he’d like.”

“Oh. That’d be…wonderful.” Suzy’s smile waivered just a bit.

I squirmed in my seat, feeling guilty for not warning Suzy. But in my shortsighted, trusting way, I had assumed Aunt Lena had called her ahead of time. I could’ve slapped myself for not knowing better.

Perusing the menu, our conversation loosened and became rather pleasant. Orders placed, I thought it would be safe for me to leave the two women alone for the time it would take me to call Jerry Wolden and get his nephew's name. It had to be faster than continuing to hunt for Gino's page three.

It took even less time than I'd hope for since he didn't answer, and I had no intention of leaving a message. I decided to try again later.

When I returned to the table, things were turning rocky. The banana chocolate chip muffin, yogurt, and diet pop I'd had were churning in my stomach.

"A form-fitting wedding dress is out, of course. Your figure is still good for your age, but tight clothes just look cheap." My aunt sat back in her chair, as if she'd just explained String Theory.

Scanning Suzy's face, I could tell she was debating her response. I jumped in, aiming to keep the peace. "It totally depends on the dress. Suzy will just have to try on a bunch of them. That's what we're here for."

Suzy insisted on picking up the check. Then we strolled from store to store until we found a place with gowns befitting a wedding. I held up a lavender above-the-knee jersey knit that would complement Suzy's figure, while Aunt Lena picked out a dark grey boxy dress that even a nun could wear without feeling guilty.

Suzy caressed the material of the dress I'd chosen. "Little too young for me. This would look great on you, Claire. And look! It's on sale." While I wondered if the stretchy material would drape over my less-than-svelte hips, Suzy pointed to the other outfit. "Lena, that's you. Do you want to try it on?"

My aunt harrumphed. "Now that I look at it, it's even a little too mature for me." She returned it to the rack.

"Well I'm going to see how this looks." I slipped into a dressing room. It fit nicely and, though, warm for mid-June, it'd be perfect for a September wedding. Relieved to have found my bridesmaid's dress with so little effort, I felt like I was on a lucky roll. I called Wolden again. This time he answered.

I kept my voice down so the other two women wouldn't hear. "Mr. Wolden, this is Claire from Francini Investigations. We handled a case for you a while back."

"What? What was that?"

A little louder, "Francini Investigation Agency."

"What do you want with them?"

"No, I'm *with* them. I have a question concerning your case?"

"Speak up. Can't hear you if you mumble."

"I'm not mumb—your nephew. Could you tell me his name?"

His voice rose. "Yes, he's my nephew. Is he in some trouble?"

I took a deep breath. "No, I just need his name."

"What'd you say? Damn phone. Can't hear anything. You still there?"

"Yes. I just need his name."

"Name? Gerald Wolden."

"Does he have the same name as you?"

"Who?"

"Your nephew." I switched the phone from one hand to the other.

"You want my nephew's name?"

"Yes, please."

He growled, "If you're really from that agency, you should know it. This is one of those scams, I can tell. Don't call this number again." He was gone.

"Urhh." I put my phone away, knowing I'd have to visit Wolden in person to get any information from him.

When I came out of the dressing room, Aunt Lena and Suzy were in a discussion by a rack of evening gowns. As I approached, my aunt held up a cream-colored V-necked dress devoid of all decoration save a small ruffle down the front. It wasn't exciting, but at least it was tasteful.

Suzy, on the other hand, held a strapless gown with tiny gold sequins dotting the front and a large ruffle down the backside. It was…eye catching. And easy to see Suzy loved it. She actually glowed when she tried on the dress. It was clearly a case of the gown looking better on than off.

My shoulders relaxed. This shopping challenge had ended on a peaceful note with Suzy and me buying the dresses we had tried on. Only Aunt Lena seemed a bit out of sorts.

I checked the time. Enough left to visit Mr. Wolden.

Ahead of my travel time estimate, I was waiting patiently at the traffic light to make a left-hand turn onto the street intersecting with Jerry Wolden's road when I glanced in the rearview mirror and stiffened. A dark blue sedan with a Smalley's bumper sticker made a right hand turn and drove past me. It looked like the car that had picked up Wolden at bingo and at the chocolate store. *Could it be Wolden and his nephew?*

As soon as the light changed, I gunned the motor and did a U-turn. Maybe I could catch up with them. But by that time, they were too far away. I slammed my hand against the steering wheel.

With less than thirty minutes to get to my sax lesson, I was tempted to call Todd and cancel so I could stake out Wolden's home. But the need for my money back was pretty strong and Todd *had* promised he'd return all of it if I wasn't happy. Right now I wasn't happy I'd had to charge the bridesmaid's dress. With the money I'd get back from Todd, I could actually pay the bill on time, rather than wait and hope Gino would reimburse me.

I began my route to Todd's music studio.

Being Saturday afternoon, it was a challenge finding a parking spot. I circled the area twice, hoping somebody had vacated their space. No luck. Then I remembered from my last session with Todd, that there was another parking area behind the stores. It was probably for the store owners only. Desperate, I swung around and drove there.

A few spaces were open but, as I thought, a sign stated they weren't for the general public. That wasn't what stopped me though. At the far end was the dark blue sedan I'd seen making the right turn earlier. And, unless I was very mistaken, the same sedan I'd seen pulling away after my first sax lesson.

My stomach tensed. *Was Todd Shotswell Jerry Wolden's nephew?*

Our conversation about a relative in the hospital rushed back to me. Jerry had collapsed and was rushed to Fairview Hospital from bingo the previous night. I knocked the back of my head against the headrest. *How could I have missed that? How did Birch fit into it?*

Only one way to find out. I disregarded the warning sign and swerved into a vacant spot, grabbed my sax and my gun and took a deep breath. I forced my reluctant feet to turn toward Todd's studio.

Chapter Twenty-Seven

"Hello, Claire." He checked his watch. "I was afraid you'd cancel on me at the last minute. I'm glad to see you didn't." He pointed to a nearby chair. "Please, have a seat so we can get started."

Funny, I just realized how long and slender his fingers were. They matched his lanky frame. Amazing how some people could escape the common middle-age spread as he had. "Thanks."

We began the lesson at the point at which we'd ended the first. With the same screeches and flat notes. I wondered how Todd could keep from covering his ears.

Fifteen minutes later, I lowered the sax and shook my head. "It's useless. My talent must lie in other areas."

"You mean other instruments? Could be. Are you interested in piano?"

"No, but maybe guitar? Know any good guitar players who might teach?" My tone was joking, but I carefully watched his reaction.

As cool and smooth as marble, he responded, "I do. But let's give the sax the whole hour. By the way, have you practiced any?"

"No. Haven't had time." I lifted my face up and caught his

eye. "I've been busy looking into some incidents that took place in Pittsburgh. About ten years ago."

I'd laid out the bait, but he didn't go near the trap. "Hmm. Let's start from the top again."

"Before we do, is there a restroom?"

He frowned then reversed it into a smile. "Of course. Go up to that hall and turn right."

Past the restroom was a storage room. Checking to make sure I was out of Todd's view, I peeked inside. As soon as my eyes adjusted to the darkness, I spotted a stack of receipts. They were addressed to Todd B. Shotswell. *B for Birch?*

I closed the door as quietly as I could and ducked into the restroom to think. My ideas were so busy bouncing off my skull I didn't hear him knocking.

"Are you all right, Claire?"

I opened the door. "Sorry."

"It's fine. I just, well, didn't want you to hide in there dreading the rest of the lesson."

My laugh sounded as brittle as uncooked fettuccini. "I'm not feeling well. Could we postpone this?"

He hesitated just a moment. "Yes, of course." Almost as an afterthought, he added, "Why don't you call me when you're feeling better?"

Acutely aware of his studying me, I fumbled as I disassembled my sax and put it away.

As I walked out the door, he called after me to take care of myself. "Don't go playing any bingo games until you feel better."

That last comment chilled me enough to need the car's heater on. Making sure Todd wasn't following me, I headed to the police station.

Corrigan listened to my rushed explanations. When I'd

finished, he scowled. "So Todd Shotswell is Jerry Wolden's nephew and he may have killed his mother. But there's no evidence. Shotswell's middle initial was 'B'. Looked it up and it *does* stand for Birch. Probably a few other guys have that same name. Although he's a good ten years younger than Eileen, let's say he did know her, but again, no evidence. And nothing indicates he lived in Pittsburgh. *Ever.* And last but not least, what's his motive?"

"Blackmail. There's no evidence he lived in Pittsburgh because he went by another name." My eyes narrowed. "Have you bothered to look at that picture of Birch? I bet anything it's a match for Todd."

Corrigan leaned back in his chair and templed his fingers. "Sure. I've looked at it." He sat forward again I suppose to show his earnestness. "Okay. I'll get the picture blown up and studied. We'll see if there's any connection between Shotswell and Birch, the guitar player. But again, even if they're the same guy, there's no evidence he's killed anyone."

"No evidence *yet*. You'll let me know as soon as you find something?"

He patted my hand. "Promise. Hey, I've got to get back to yet another anonymous tip. I'll call you later."

Feeling somewhat defeated, I returned to my car and then to Charlie and my apartment. At least my dog would listen to my ideas without thinking I'd gone off the deep end.

***

Here it was, Saturday evening and I was eating leftover pizza with Charlie as my date. He was a lousy dinner partner, since he kept leaving his food bowl to beg for some of my meal. I finally gave in and tossed him a piece of the melted-then-hardened cheese. He chewed it and then spit it out. Even he had higher standards.

As a reward for finishing the leftovers, I scrounged in my freezer and came up with half a chocolate chunk peanut butter cookie. No idea where the other half had gone.

I defrosted it and sat at my computer, working the facts in the Red Bow Killer cases.

Say Todd was *the* Birch. After all, he was a musician and had known ties to at least some of the victims, besides Eileen. Eileen was probably blackmailing him, but what was it about the ribbon and why kill all those other women? Even his uncle didn't trust him. Why? I had no answers. The same doubts Corrigan had formed an unending circle in my brain.

Tired of questions without answers, I picked up Charlie's leash for one last stroll outside. He jumped up, wagging his tail and trotting to the door. With my gun and keys in hand, we stepped out into the hallway.

Down the sidewalk we strolled. I coaxed Charlie to stop sniffing everything and do what needed to be done. At long last, he complied and then back up the stairs we went.

My mind still occupied with Todd Birch Shotswell, I unlocked my door and was about to step inside when footsteps echoed through the hallway.

A loud, "Claire." It was Todd. Now almost right behind me.

What's he doing here? I wanted to dash inside my apartment and bolt the door, but my feet felt stuck to the hallway carpet.

He wore an apologetic smile. "I would've called you, but I couldn't read the phone number you gave me. Something came up with the relative I told you about and I'm going to have to close the studio for a while. Given the circumstances, I think the fairest thing I can do is refund your money like we discussed." He removed a check from his pocket and held it out to me.

For a moment, I let my guard down. As I reached for the check, he grabbed my wrist and yanked so hard I thought he'd dislocated it. A second later he had me in a choke hold, dragging me into my apartment.

He attempted to slam the door after us, but Charlie leaped inside and came to my defense, plunging his teeth into Todd's trousers. Todd, trying to get loose, shook his leg hard, but Charlie hung on.

My dear dog's effort was enough to knock Todd off balance and I escaped his grip. I elbowed my assailant in the gut, whipped around and had my gun on him before he could take a breath.

I called off Charlie, who released Todd, but continued growling at the man.

My breaths came in pants, synchronized with Charlie's. "Sit down, Todd." Watching him closely, I felt around for my purse, hoping to grab my phone.

His soulless eyes followed my moves, making me clumsy. I fumbled and lost my hold on my purse. The phone slipped out, and for just a second, I foolishly glanced down so I could grab it. That was all Todd needed to leap up and try to wrestle the gun from my sweaty hand. In our struggle, my phone slid out of reach.

Charlie again sprang into action, valiantly nipping and barking at Todd, while the killer and I grappled for the gun. His vicious kick to Charlie landed and my poor brave pup lay there whimpering. He was going to pay for hurting my dog. I let out a Braveheart-like war cry and dug the nails of my free hand into Todd's face.

He released a guttural sound and slapped me hard with his left hand.

Reeling from the blow, my grip slipped from the gun. The weapon was now his alone.

He snarled, "Okay, Claire, your turn to sit down." He pushed me hard and I stumbled back onto the sofa. Keeping the gun on me, he tore off the tie he was wearing and bound my hands.

After he was done, he leaned against the wall across from me. "You know, this isn't how I'd wanted this."

"You didn't want to kill me?"

"Yes, of course. From the first time you came into my studio I knew you weren't really interested in saxophone lessons. So I did my research. You're a private investigator. My uncle hired your firm to investigate me. But I turned the tables. I have to admit, stalking, but not harming you made it interesting. Even breaking into your apartment was exhilarating, leaving you a clue, teasing you."

That half of a cookie I'd eaten soured in my belly. I should have called the cops that night.

He continued, sounding almost regretful. "But the fun has to end and I have to kill you now. But it's really not my fault. You know, it's Eileen's. All of this."

"What do you mean?" The longer we talked, the better my chances of staying alive. "Because she was blackmailing you?"

He tsk'd. "She wasn't blackmailing me." His face softened. "We were going to get married. I wasn't good at saving, so every week I gave her part of the money I made with the band. We were putting it toward our wedding."

"But what happened?"

He released a short, bitter laugh. "She said I could trust her with anything and I believed her, until the night we were celebrating. I had too much to drink. I told her about the women, what I'd done. I promised her I wouldn't do it again. But she wouldn't listen. Turned out, she was just like all the others."

My head was buzzing. "The other women?"

His upper lip curled. "Selfish pigs. All of them. They deserved to die. Just like my mother. Just like Eileen."

My voice quivered. "What did they do that was so bad?" I took a stab at the answer. "Play bingo?"

He waved the gun around and I could feel my heart batting against my chest, terrified the weapon would go off. "Yes. Bingo!" His brow lowered and he snarled, "My dear mother left me, a 12-year-old, to take care of my sick father. She was too busy with bingo. He died while she was playing. On his birthday. Which also happened to be my birthday. She had to pay, so I killed her. Tied a red bow around her neck as a present to him. And to me." An icy smile passed across his lips. "Just like all the women after her. Presents for both of us. The red bow is a nice touch, don't you think?"

Struggling to keep my hysteria at bay, I asked, "But Rose didn't even play bingo."

He waved my comment away saying, "A bar fly who couldn't stay away from musicians."

"But—"

He ignored my objection and continued with his own narrative. "I stopped when Eileen and I got engaged. Since the cops charged someone else for the murders, we had a clean slate. But she still ran away from me and my secret." He rubbed his temple with his free hand. "I had to find her and kill her too." Dreamily, he added, "It was a sweet reunion."

Keep him talking. "How did you get out of the concert to kill Mrs. Amato? You were playing the clarinet in front of an audience."

Dripping with smugness, he answered, "After the intermission, I switched to the piano. For the first two overtures, I didn't play and the lights weren't on me. I had enough time to do what needed to be done. Vincenza's house was only five minutes away."

I wanted to squeeze the life out of him. Instead, I tried persuasion. "You made up for your dad's death. I'm sure he wouldn't want you to keep killing, especially not after all this time."

"Stop talking." Todd cocked the gun, aiming it at my head. Beads of sweat popped out from his temples. "You don't know what he suffered. Those women I killed deserved to die." His face brightened. "You'll be the last. Then I'll leave town. Close the shop. Nothing left to hold me here. Not even my uncle." *Had he killed Jerry too?*

My eyes darted around the room and I'd wished I'd taught Charlie how to call 911. "Why don't you start with a clean slate now? I won't say a word about what you told me. Besides, I don't even play bingo." I was bargaining with the devil.

With a phony sad smile he said, "It doesn't matter, Claire. You know too much." With his free hand, he extracted a red ribbon from his pants pocket.

I was desperate and trembling all over. But I had to keep my wits about me. "If you shoot me, I'll bleed all over the ribbon and spoil the present."

He moved closer until he was almost on top of me. "I'm not going to shoot you. Not unless I have to."

From the corner of my eye, I saw Charlie rise and with one final effort, he jumped onto Todd. The dog was too weak to do any damage, but it was enough to make Todd lose his footing, giving me the opportunity to ram my head into him.

We tumbled onto the ground together, the gun slipping from his hand. I kicked at him, fighting for my life.

My strength was almost gone, and it was clear without my hands I couldn't win this battle. Then I spotted the saxophone case half-hidden under the sofa. A lucky knee to Todd's groin gave me the chance to drop down. I scratched at the case until I could grab hold of it. With my last burst of energy, I yanked the heavy thing out with both hands, swung it and connected with the side of Todd's head.

He fell over, unconscious, but his chest continued to rise and fall. I darted into the kitchen for my butcher knife and rubbed it against the tie. As soon as I was able to free my hands, I called the police.

After that, I turned that piece of human trash over and bound his hands with Charlie's leash. Then, grabbing a pair of my tights, I tied his ankles.

I could hear the wailing of the police sirens when Todd, still groggy, awoke. With my gun focused on him, I couldn't help myself. "So Rose liked musicians. Some of the other victims played instruments. What was so bad about that?"

He grimaced. "Did I tell you my mother was also a musician?"

There was so much more I wanted to ask, but from the sound of the sirens the police were close.

He coughed. "Claire, before they get here, could I have some water? Please?"

Grudgingly, but seeing no harm in it, I went into the kitchen and opened the cupboard to get a glass. I set the gun down to turn the water on. The glass was half full when I was jerked back. Todd had the cold blade of a knife against my neck.

"You should've searched me for other weapons, Claire."

I stood deathly still. "The cops are almost here. Put the knife down, Todd."

With a sinister laugh he said, "We'll go together."

I threw the water in his face. He stepped backwards and tripped over my wonderful, brave dog. With that jarring motion, the knife slipped, leaving a ribbon of pain across my shoulder.

Todd lunged at me, subhuman rage in his eyes.

I spun around, grabbed my gun and shot him. The bullet pushed him back a bit as it entered his upper arm. He wasn't deterred. Jaw locked, his eyes hard, he came at me again.

Knowing this was my last chance to live, I pulled the trigger again.

Frankenstein-like, he lurched at me, then stumbled and collapsed. He was dead.

When I bent over Todd, a drop of blood splattered onto his arm. My blood. My hand flew up to my throbbing shoulder and came away crimson.

"This is the police. Open up." I grabbed a towel and made it to the door just before they broke it down.

The officers went about their business while the EMT's examined me. Luckily Todd's slash to my shoulder was long, but not deep enough to require anything more than bandaging.

But my poor brave Charlie was hurt. Unfortunately the cops told me I had to give my statement before I could leave.

I was frantic. "But my dog needs a vet! Now!" One of the emergency rescuers took pity on me and called a 24 hour animal clinic. They'd see Charlie as soon as I could get him there.

Less than three minutes later, Corrigan busted into my apartment, his face wild with worry. As soon as he spotted me, he rushed to my side. Pulling me to him, he whispered,

"Thank God you're okay."

"Me too." Was all I could think to say.

Then remembering himself, he dropped his arms and cleared his throat. "I'll need your statement."

Leaving nothing out, I ended my report to Corrigan with, "Todd was the Red Bow Killer. All because his mother played bingo instead of taking care of Todd's father."

"He didn't limit it just to women. We found Jerry Wolden's body. Looks like Shotswell killed him too. Oh, by the way, the photo helped us ID Shotswell. He went by the name of Birch Wilson in Pittsburgh. But he may have been responsible for a number of unsolved deaths before then. We're still investigating."

"Yeah, he told me about killing the women in Pittsburgh. What about his last victim? The woman he left alive?"

"She's responding to simple commands. The doctors think she'll recover fully. If so, she can corroborate your information."

Corrigan closed his notepad and stuck it in his jacket pocket. Then he leaned over and wrapped my hands in his larger ones. "I wish this hadn't happened to you. I wish you weren't determined to put yourself in harm's way all the time. But I'm glad you're okay and," He took a deep breath, "I'm so proud of you."

I felt like the Cowardly Lion being told he was brave. My face must have glowed. I thought I'd never hear those words from him. I even temporarily forgot the pain from the cut on my shoulder.

Chapter Twenty-Eight

It was only the middle of September and the leaves had already turned red and yellow with some cascading down onto the lawns and streets. Luckily the weather hadn't taken its final turn toward autumn and the temperature was projected to be in the upper 60's. Perfect for my dad's wedding.

My jersey knit bridesmaid's dress fit perfectly. None of the unsightly bulges that had concerned me when I bought the outfit. Suzy had trimmed and thinned my thick hair and showed me how to wear the flower clip. I had to admit, the piece was a nice contrast to my dark strands.

Charlie nuzzled me in an attempt to get me to stay home with him. He'd had several fractured ribs courtesy of Todd Shotswell, but after two and a half months he was up and about. I rewarded his valor by signing him up for a toy-a-month club.

I picked up my purse and headed toward the door. After the investigation, I'd received the $10,000 reward for Eileen's killer. I gave half of it to Gino. Only fair. I couldn't have linked all the clues together without him. Plus that allowed him to pay off Griselli without Betty knowing.

First time I'd ever seen Gino at a loss for words.

By the time I arrived at Suzy's house, three other cars were already parked in the driveway. Inside, my aunt was barking orders like a drill sergeant with a hangover. "Don't sit down! You'll ruin the line of the dress."

Despite these and other admonishments from my family and from an older cousin of Suzy's I didn't even know she had, Suzy looked radiant. And calm.

When I marveled at her serenity, she whispered to me, "When you're a hairdresser, you learn to take everything in your stride."

Ed, who had agreed to drive the bridal party to the church, was standing on the sidelines cracking his knuckles. I caught his eye and he grinned.

Finally, we were all herded into the car and were on our way. Aunt Lena insisted on sitting in the back, claiming the front's bucket seat would further wrinkle her dark crepe dress with its full skirt.

I volunteered for the front seat and Ed and I began an easy banter. We were sitting at a red light when he asked, "So have you signed the contract for your new office yet?" He chuckled, "Can't believe you're going to call the agency DeNardo and Son."

Putting on a fake look of outrage I responded, "Charlie's like a son to me and he did help save me. Who knows if I'd have survived Shotswell's attack without his help?"

He chortled, "Guess it's okay. As long as I don't have to depend on him signing my checks." Ed had agreed to be a part time investigator when the DeNardo and Son agency was up and running.

A short time later, we arrived at the back of the church so Dad wouldn't be able to see Suzy until she walked down the aisle. But I spotted Corrigan, looking dashingly handsome with his blond hair and his cut-away tux. He was helping my father with his tie so didn't see me. Whether it was how gorgeous Corrigan looked or seeing my dad dressed for his wedding, I don't know. But a lump the size of a meatball rose in my throat.

The wedding, with Father Gilbert presiding, was lovely. The bride and groom looked so happy, even Aunt Lena forgot to worry out loud. Immediately afterwards, there was a small reception at Terrino's Hall. Although my aunt didn't cater it, she and Angie had made the cake, a wonderful strawberries and custard affair. Even nicer, all the guests, as favors, received miniature chocolate chip cupcakes with strawberry frosting. I wondered if she had any extras.

The bride was just about to toss her bouquet when my phone rang. It was the realtor about my bid on the office and I had to take the call.

Just as well. I'd caught a bouquet at the last wedding and still had no ring on my finger. I slipped into the restroom to hear better.

"I'm so sorry, Claire. The owner decided to take the

office off the market." The woman on the other end didn't sound as sorry as I felt. "But we'll keep looking. We'll find something in your budget."

After accepting, but not believing her words of encouragement, I left the restroom to return to all the smiling faces. But before I could get back into the reception room, Gino stopped me.

"Nice wedding. Your dad looks real happy."

I forced a smile. "Yes they both do. Have you and Betty set a date?"

He lowered his voice. "That's what I want to talk to you about."

Surely he wouldn't want me to be his best man. "Is something wrong?"

"No. it's just…How would you like to own Francini's?"

"What?" Maybe I needed my hearing checked.

"Betty and me have decided to move to Florida. Miami. I know you been looking for your own agency. Now you don't have to."

I tamped down on any excitement. "But I've only got $4,000." I withheld some for changes I'd need to make.

He gave a short nod. "That would be all we'd need to get us hitched and down to Miami. What do you say?"

My voice quivered with excitement. "I'd say, yes."

He grabbed my hand and shook it. Then he gave me a quick hug. "Congratulations! You own Francini's. We can draw up the contract Monday." He stopped pumping my hand. "Are you changing the name? I'll take the sign if you are. You never know."

I smiled. "Go ahead and take the sign. Now we better get back to the festivities. They're throwing the bouquet."

"Thanks. Betty says she's not going for the flowers. Says she'll leave it for the unclaimed women."

"Unclaimed? What are we, lost and found items?"

He shrugged and when he did so, we both heard a roar of laughter followed by cheers.

We both lit out for the reception room. There was Corrigan, holding both the garter and the bouquet.

I started to say something, but he grabbed me by the arm and dragged me outside the hall. "I figured I wasn't taking any chances, so I went for the bouquet too." He handed the flowers to me.

My eyes widened and I clutched the flowers tightly as he got down on one knee. His voice cracked, "Claire DeNardo, will you marry me?"

I threw my arms around his neck and giggled. Between the giggles, I believe I said yes.

The End

Recipes…

Lemon Chicken with Olives and Potatoes

My mother used to make a dish similar to the following one. When I went on my own, I tweaked it a bit to my taste. Feel free to do your own tweaking.

8 bone-in, skin-on chicken thighs

Kosher salt and ground black pepper to taste

3 tablespoons olive oil

2-4 garlic cloves, smashed

1 large yellow or white onion, sliced thinly

4 medium potatoes cut into 1" pieces

2 tablespoons fresh oregano

2 lemons, thinly sliced, seeds removed

1 large sprig rosemary

1 tablespoon fresh thyme

1 1/3 cups chicken stock

1 cup pitted green and kalamata olives

1 tablespoon all-purpose flour

- *Preheat oven to 350 degrees F. Pat chicken thighs dry with a paper towel and season liberally on both sides.*
- *In a large ovenproof pan or Dutch oven large enough to hold all thighs in a single layer, heat the oil over medium-high heat. When the oil is hot, add the chicken, skin side down and sear until golden brown, 5 to 6 minutes. Add the garlic to the pan and flip the chicken over. Cook until the garlic is a little brown, 2 to 3 minutes. Remove the chicken and garlic from the pan and set aside.*
- *Add onions to the pan and sauté 1 to 2 minutes.*
- *Add potatoes, olives, garlic, oregano, and thyme. Stir to combine. Cook and stir occasionally for 4 to 5 minutes.*
- *Sprinkle flour over the onions and potatoes and stir.*

- *Pour in chicken stock and stir. Nestle the chicken thighs into the pan and tuck the lemon slices among the chicken and vegetables. Add the rosemary sprig.*
- *Cover the pan and bake 40 minutes, until the potatoes are tender and the chicken is cooked through. Remove the rosemary stem.*

And for dessert, try a spin on Aunt Lena's cupcakes…

Strawberry Filled Chocolate Chip Cupcakes

I like these cupcakes plain, but if I'm in a *calories-don't-matter* mood, I top the baked beauties with the strawberry frosting included at the end of this recipe. Make the filling first so it has time to cool completely.

Filling:

1 cup water

2 ½ cups frozen strawberries, thawed and cut into bite sized pieces

3 tablespoons cornstarch

¾ cups granulated sugar

Directions:

- *Whisk water and cornstarch together.*
- *Stir in strawberries and sugar.*
- *Cook over medium heat, stirring occasionally until thick, about 10 minutes.*

Cupcake:

1/3 cup butter (room temperature)

1 cup granulated sugar

1 large egg (room temperature)

2 cups cake flour

½ teaspoon salt

2 ½ teaspoons baking powder

¾ cups whole milk

1 teaspoon vanilla

1 cup mini chocolate chips

- *Preheat oven to 350 degrees F. Line the cupcake pan with cupcake liners.*
- *In a mixer, cream together the butter and sugar until smooth.*
- *Add the egg and beat again.*
- *In separate bowl, mix flour, salt, and baking powder. Set aside.*
- *In another bowl, mix milk, oil and vanilla.*
- *Alternate the dry ingredients with the wet ones in the butter-sugar-egg mixture. Beat thoroughly after each addition.*
- *Fold in chocolate chips.*
- *Fill cupcake liners 1/3 full. Add 1 tablespoon of the strawberry mixture, topping that with another dollop of batter until the liner is 2/3 full.*
- *Bake 20-30 minutes or until toothpick comes out clean from center of the cupcake.*

Strawberry Frosting (Optional):

1 (8 ounce) package cream cheese, softened

¼ cup butter, room temperature

½ granulated sugar

1 cup strawberries, chopped

1 tablespoon lemon juice

- *In electric mixer, beat cream cheese and butter until smooth.*
- *Gradually add in sugar until mix is again smooth.*
- *Add strawberries and lemon juice. Beat until everything is combined.*
- *Spread on cupcakes*

Terrified Detective Series

***Plateful of Murder*:**

Claire DeNardo is scared of a lot of things. Ordinary objects like roller coasters and men's hairpieces make her knees knock loud enough to be a band's rhythm section. Unfortunately, the only job Claire can find is working for her Uncle Gino in his seedy detective agency. Until now, her cases have all be middle-aged men with trophy wives who needed watching. But when Gino retires and leaves her in charge, Claire gets swept up in a murder case despite her fears. Both the client who hired her and the handsome police detective want her off the case. When the wrong person is charged, it's up to the terrified detective to summon all the courage she can to find the true killer.